BOOKS BY PHYLLIS REYNOLDS NAYLOR

Witch's Sister
Witch Water
The Witch Herself
Walking Through the Dark
How I Came to Be a Writer
How Lazy Can You Get?
Eddie, Incorporated
All Because I'm Older
Shadows on the Wall
Faces in the Water
Footprints at the Window
The Boy With the Helium Head
A String of Chances

A String of Chances

A String of
Chances

Phyllis Reynolds Naylor

Atheneum   New York   1983

LIBRARY OF CONGRESS CATALOGING IN PUBLICATION DATA

Naylor, Phyllis Reynolds.
  A string of chances.

  SUMMARY: *During the summer she spends with a
married cousin, the sixteen-year-old daughter of a small
town preacher not only discovers secrets which divide her
family, but experiences, for the first time, uncertainties
about her life and beliefs.*
  [1. Family life—Fiction] I. Title.
PZ7.N24St   [Fic]   82-1790
ISBN 0-689-30935-X   AACR2

To my grandfather, John S. Reynolds,
whom I loved, but never really knew

A String of Chances

One

THAT BOY WOULD BE sleeping in her room come Sunday. The moment Evie moved out, in fact, Matt Jewel was moving in. Her parents seemed to pick up people like stray kittens on the side of the road.

"A bit of the devil, he is," Aunt Ida grumbled when she heard about it, for Matt's name had become a household word by the time he left Branbury.

"Looking meek as baby Moses, but acting like Matt Jewel," Mother might say about a pupil in her Bible class.

Or, when the hired man gave her any lip, Evie's sister, Rose, would huff, "Murphy's stubborn as Matt Jewel, I swear it!"

Only Father held his tongue. "We're all of us here for a purpose," he told them once, to which Aunt Ida replied,

"Yes, anyone can serve, if only as a horrible example."

Matt was only half the problem, Evie mused as she bumped open the door to the dining room and took the tray inside. Nobody came right out and said it: *Evie, don't go.* But they must have been doing a powerful lot of thinking because the vibrations were so strong sometimes they almost made her teeth rattle.

She crossed the floor to the bed, which had been placed near the bay window. Beneath his shaggy brows, an old man watched as she set the tray on his lap. It was his wild glare that she found unnerving, for the eyes never stopped staring at her from the moment she entered his room.

A few more days and you'll have Matt Jewel to stare at, she thought as she took her usual seat in the rocker, letting her straight yellow hair hang down over the back.

Aloud, she said, "School's out, and I'll be leaving this weekend, Mr. Schmidt. My cousin's expecting a baby, and I'm staying with her this summer."

The huge eyes didn't even blink.

She tried to catch him off-guard—would glance away and then look back—hoping she might find him studying the meat loaf there on his plate. The ear of corn was supposed to be a treat.

"It's from the freezer," Evie told him as she saw his gnarled fingers search it out, but his dark eyes never left her face, and she looked away, finding it impossible to stare him down. *Talk to him*, her mother had said. *Who knows how much that poor soul understands.*

"A boy's coming here while I'm gone," Evie continued, addressing the china cupboard where the cut-glass plates and saucers had become relics from disuse. Her voice took on the rhythm of the rocker. "It's been seven years since I saw him. We were both nine, and he locked me in the broom closet at church—said if I prayed hard enough, Jesus would let me out." Evie could tell that the old man had stopped chewing and seemed to be listening intently; then the chewing resumed. "Well, it was Dad who let me out, and I was so mad at Matt Jewel I cried. He and his mother moved to Waldorf, and I'd be happy never to see him again, if you want the truth."

She glanced toward the old man and realized he had eaten the corn and was chewing on the cob.

"No, Mr. Schmidt," she said, going over to the bed. She tried wrestling it gently away from him, but his teeth and hands hung on.

"Mother!" Evie yelled.

There were footsteps in the pantry, and then the door to the dining room swung open. Mrs. Hutchins stepped up to the bed. She wore her gray hair short and casual and had a pleasant no-nonsense look on her face:

"Now, Mr. Schmidt, you don't want that when I've a pudding waiting," she said and, deftly prying the cob free, dropped it in the pocket of her smock.

"You should have watched him, Evelyn," Aunt Ida said in the kitchen. "The man will eat his napkin and plate if you're not looking every second."

A zoo, that's what we've got! Rose had exploded last year when Sister Ozzie was added to the family. *We've got an aphasic, a retarded, and now a senile old lady who acts like a duchess. Any morning I expect to wake up and find someone's taken over my room.*

Evie silently thrust her arms down into the dishwater, glancing now and then in the little mirror tacked above the sink, just under the plaque that read, "It is not when a man dies that matters, but rather what dies inside a man while he lives." She always imagined somebody walking around with a dead spleen or something. Her eyes began to crinkle a little at the corners, and she studied her face as she absently washed the silverware. The skin was smooth, like eggshell, but there were pointy cheekbones on either side. Yuk. She would look like Aunt Ida when she was older, she was sure of it.

" 'Bout the last time we can expect your help with the dishes, I reckon." Aunt Ida was drying the plates, and she slung them one at a time into the cupboard as though she were dealing cards. That, Evie was certain, was something her aunt had never done.

"I'll have plenty to do at Donna Jean's," Evie told her. "Once that baby comes, most likely I'll have the cooking to do and the cleaning up after."

"It's not like she didn't have a husband," Rose put in. "Seems to me Tom could help her some. Lots of women have babies and don't need a live-in maid for three months."

"I'm not going there as a maid; I'm going as a friend," Evie said.

Aunt Ida shuffled over to the stove, grabbed the gravy pan and plunked it down in the sink. "Well, it just don't look right, if you ask me—a young girl like you going off to sleep under the same roof with them."

Evie glanced at her. "Tom Rawley isn't the least bit interested in me, if that's what you're worried about; Donna Jean's got a whole lot more to pinch than I have."

Both Aunt Ida and Rose turned around.

"Now that's the kind of talk, young lady, that leads to trouble," Aunt Ida said.

Evie drew in her breath, held it, then let it out. *Sheesh!* They should hear the way the kids talked at school! Now that she was sixteen, little mannerisms of her family had begun to irritate her. Maybe she was simply growing up. Growing *away*,

Mother had put it, voicing her fears about Evie's plans for the summer.

"I'm going," Evie said grimly, and the face in the mirror stared back. Her eyes were deepset, so that there was the brow and then the eye, with hardly any space in between, and her lips were thin, not at all the type she could put great globs of lipstick on, even if she wanted to.

Like one of those Tennessee mountain women, Rose had said of her once. Evie did not resemble Rose much at all, but rather her other sister, Wilma. Yet it was Wilma, thin-nosed and plain, who married, and Rose, beautiful Rose, who stayed behind.

There was rain that evening—sheets of it, like walls of water, holding them prisoner. Evie and a friend had gone up-county to the K-Mart, and now they stood inside the glass doors waiting for Sue Shields' mother to pick them up. Along with tee shirts and records, Evie had not been able to resist a toy kitten that squeaked when she squeezed it, just right for one corner of a newborn's bed.

Across the street, the lights of the arcade flashed and whirled, spots of color reflecting off the wet pavement. Rock music blared.

"We should have told her we'd be waiting over there," Sue said.

"I'm not allowed," Evie told her.

"We could at least stand in the doorway."

"What for?"

"To see who's in there." Sue passed over the sack of chocolate-covered raisins. She was shorter than Evie and looked out at the world through blue-tinted glasses that made her eyes appear sultry, even when she was wearing cut-offs. "Maybe you'd see the guy you told me about—the one who's coming to live at your place this summer."

"Oh, him. I wouldn't care if he was."

"Well, it's creepy, if you ask me. Some boy staying in your room. . . . What if he gets in your stuff?"

"What stuff?"

"Your clothes and things."

"Sue Shields, you're crazier than crazy! Why would he want to get in my clothes? You talk like my folks just take in any queer kind of person who comes along." Somehow her voice was unconvincing.

Sue squatted down, her back against the wall. "It's weird. I wouldn't want some guy sleeping in my bedroom. What about love letters?"

"I don't have any."

"Not even from Clyde Harrigan?"

Evie pretended to throw up in her shirt pocket.

They watched the rain stream down the glass, and suddenly Sue asked, "Why do they do it—take in folks like that?"

Evie had never really considered it. As long as

she could remember, there had been extra people in the Hutchinses' home. Her parents just did, that's all. Certainly not for the small fee that Sister Ozzie paid them from her social security or the stipend from the county that helped cover Mr. Schmidt's care. . . . *that they may see your good works and glorify your Father which is in heaven*, Mr. Hutchins often said, quoting the Scriptures, and Evie figured that explained it.

"It says to in the Bible," she told Sue.

She was never sure just how much Sue, being Methodist, understood, because people in her father's church—Faith Gospel—had their own way of doing things, and there weren't too many of them around. She always considered it some sort of miracle that her parents had found each other in the first place—the preacher and the practical nurse. What fateful set of circumstances had brought her father up from Georgia and her mother over from Richmond to meet in the town of Mason Springs and move at last to Branbury? What was it, in fact, that had brought Wilma and the man she had married together, or Donna Jean and Tom?

"Sue," she said, "are you ever going to have a baby?"

"I don't know. Sometimes I think I'll just adopt. Are you?"

"If I didn't, I'd probably regret it. Our mare had a colt last week, though, and she was huge. I was there when Murphy delivered her—all those legs sticking out. I kept thinking about Donna Jean."

"Well, here's how I see it: if it was really awful, women wouldn't go on having babies. They'd have one and stop."

"Yeah, you're right. Mother was midwife to a woman last year who already had thirteen children. She asked her if she didn't think fourteen was enough, and the woman said she'd stop when God quit sending them."

"Gross."

"Sometimes I think, well, women have to have the babies and men have to fight the wars. Maybe it all evens out."

"There's Mother. . . ."

A car had pulled up across the street and Mrs. Shields tapped the horn. The girls flung open the glass doors and went shrieking through the downpour, stepping in ankle-deep puddles and grabbing each other for balance.

A group of young men in the doorway of the arcade whistled.

"Careful, baby," one called as Evie almost tripped on the curb.

She looked up at the grinning faces and realized that even if Matt Jewel was among them, she probably wouldn't recognize him—not after seven years.

* * *

On Saturday there was a sense of doing everything for the last time—for the summer, anyway. Evie moved about the house with special attention to the dusting, knowing that she would not have to do it again until September.

She carefully cleaned the upstairs. Her sister's room was perfectly arranged, with matching print bedspread and curtains. Life, however, had certainly not arranged itself the way Rose seemed to feel that it should. When Wilma married at seventeen—to a man with "no roots at all, to speak of," as Aunt Ida put it—Rose had called it a slap in the face, said that the younger daughters were supposed to have the decency to wait until the oldest one was married. To Evie, that sounded like something out of *Pride and Prejudice*. It was enough that couples found each other at all without having to do it in the proper sequence, and she didn't much blame Wilma for just running off and getting married in Baltimore.

The Hutchinses' house was a strange mishmash of brick and white siding, with rooms tacked on to accommodate the parade of elderly and disabled who came and went. Rose and Evie had the two bedrooms upstairs.

Evie had just run the dust mop over the floor in her sister's closet when Mother came in with fresh laundry.

"I'm going to miss having you around this summer, Evie," she said. Then, "Are you really sure you want to go?"

Evie paused. If only they wouldn't keep asking. It was as though she were going somewhere unsafe, somewhere foreign. "Donna Jean and I have been talking about it for six months," she said in answer.

Mrs. Hutchins gave her a quick hug as she crossed the room. "Well, I guess if your mind is made up, I can't stop you."

"Why would you *want* to?" Evie asked. It seemed that somehow they had all been communicating in code—the looks, the silences, the sighs. . . .

"I guess . . . I just want you to come back the same girl you are now."

They were closer to the truth, but still circling.

"What on earth could happen to me in three months?" Evie asked.

This time her mother looked her full in the face and the brow was knit just a little, three small furrows above the nose. "Evie, a lot can happen to us in only three *days*."

"Don't you trust the Rawleys?"

Mother laughed the question aside. "Even more, I trust you. Maybe it will be a good experience after all, getting away."

Evie listened to her mother's footsteps back out in the hall. Why couldn't she come right out and say it—that she and Aunt Ida and Father were worried sick about Evie's living in a godless household for three months—that Evie might return a heathen?

According to Aunt Ida, there were only two kinds of people in the world—the saved and the unsaved—and the whole point of life was getting yourself safely through the Last Judgment. *No one knows when He will come*, she often said. *No one knows when He will divide the sheep from the goats.* You had to be ready.

Evie took the dust mop out to shake it, then walked on back to the pasture to see the colt once more before she left. When she was younger, she had worried a lot about the Last Judgment. The possibilities were unlimited. She might be out on the swing when it happened, or even in the bathtub, when suddenly this big trumpet. . . . And where would the Saviour land? Probably the parking lot outside Hollander's store, and she had imagined the way people would look when they walked outside and saw God sitting there. If everybody who had ever lived rose up and came, how long would the line be? Certainly as far as Washington. . . .

She climbed the fence and made her way through the clover, drinking in the heady smell of early June. She had never worried that God would send her to hell because the worst thing she had done so far was let Clyde Harrigan put his hand under her sweater back in eighth grade, and she'd already asked God to forgive her for that. But she used to worry that when the Saviour rose toward heaven with all the Blessed, someone left below might grab her heels and hold on. Being Blessed, would it be okay for her to kick? Or would God have to start the Ascension all over?

She smiled now at the memory, but it brought back an uneasiness she had been feeling for some time. An uncertainty she had not dared speak about, even to her father. Especially her father. *Love your enemies*, Christ had said. Who invented hell, then? That was the question that bothered her. If God, who was perfect, couldn't forgive, how could He expect it of common ordinary people?

The colt stood up against its mother, with the mare's head draped protectively over his neck. Evie murmured to them as she approached, and when she sensed that the mare was willing, caressed the silky mane of the new foal, admiring the gold eyelashes, the pink underlip, feeling the steamy warmth of its body. God's creature too, but it never had to bother a bit about grace and glory, never gave a thought about hell.

She ate her lunch under the beech tree at the top of the drive. From the glider she could look down the long hill to the azalea garden along the road.

Murphy came hesitantly down the path with his own plate and cup, and Evie patted the place beside her.

"Sit here," she called.

He beamed as he always did when someone was kind—gentle, retarded Murphy—who had been with the family even before Evie was born. His mouth worked at the words before he spoke them, sometimes dragging out the first syllable as though his lips had to wrench them away.

"G . . . oing to have me a sandwich and go m . . . end the fence." He sat down gingerly.

"Nothing's going to get through that fence this afternoon," Evie told him. "The cow's so old she wouldn't even know how to step over."

Murphy grinned some more. "So old you have to w . . . alk her to water," he said, and they laughed at their joke. He took a bite and, as he chewed, picked up the small pieces of ham that fell from his lips, cramming them back in his mouth.

"I'm going away tomorrow," Evie said, wondering if he remembered. Once, when Mother had gone to Richmond and nobody thought to tell Murphy, he had sulked all week. "Donna Jean's invited me to spend the summer."

"I know it," he said. "That boy is coming." One rough hand moved down and wiped itself on his trouser leg.

"Yes. Dad wants Matt to help you out this summer."

"N . . . ever needed no help before."

"I think Dad figures you can help Matt as much

as he can help you. He needs something to keep him busy."

Murphy beamed once more and then, as Rose came down the path, got up abruptly and took his plate to the kitchen. She sat down where Murphy had been.

Her slim, birdlike legs were stretched out in front of her, feet crossed at the ankles. Despite her thinness, Rose, at twenty-four, was the prettiest one of the Hutchinses' daughters. She had the dark hair and olive complexion of her father's side of the family, the almond-shaped eyes, the full lips. It seemed there had been a time, when Rose was in high school, that she had had lots of friends, lots of boys coming around. But she didn't date now. Evie could never understand it.

Lord, I'm tired, Evie predicted.

"Lord, I'm so tired!" said Rose, and dangled one hand over the arm of the glider.

If it's not one thing, it's another, Evie thought next.

"If it's not one thing, it's another," said Rose.

Evie smiled to herself. They should go on tour. The famous Hutchins sisters in a mind-boggling demonstration of ESP.

"Why don't you go somewhere this weekend?" Evie suggested.

Rose turned her head and her eyebrows arched. "I just said I'm *tired*."

"Well, sometimes a person needs to do something different for a change."

"I ought to know what I need and when I'm tired."

Evie continued pushing her feet against the ground, and Rose allowed herself to be rocked.

"Skinny old legs," Rose said, lifting up one foot and holding it out in front of her. "A walking scarecrow, that's what I am."

Evie was always amazed at the number of pretty girls who thought there was something wrong with them. She had noticed the appreciative way the young men looked at Rose in church, but whenever she'd mentioned this to her sister, Rose would say, "Gawking at me, that's all. *Elbows like ice picks*, is what they're thinking." It was as though, when Rose looked in the mirror, she saw something different.

"You all packed?" Rose asked.

"Not quite. Figure I'll only need jeans and things."

"Well, I cerainly can't say that *I'm* going to enjoy the summer." Rose was sounding more like Aunt Ida every day, and when the two of them got together, Evie's father said once, it was *hopelessness on one side and despair on the other, both having a go at it*. "One more day and we'll have Matt Jewel wandering around the place. Dad must have been crazy to hire him."

"Maybe Matt's changed," Evie offered.

"Huh! Mother talked to Mrs. Jewel last week. Smart-alecky, his mother says. Knows it all. Tell the boy the sun will rise tomorrow and he'll even argue with that."

"Do you remember that time he put an alarm clock in Dad's pulpit?" Evie said. "And it went off after Dad had been preaching for twenty-five minutes?"

She recalled the curious look on her father's face as he had opened the door under the pulpit, the way his eyes had crinkled as he held up the clock and said that the Lord must be trying to tell him something.

"Matt ought to have been whipped," Rose declared. "It was old Mr. Kimball's funeral, though, that was the worst. The way Matt hid down under the drapes beneath the coffin and knocked three times during the service. Oh, he thought he was so clever—the way he smirked when they dragged him out. What a shock that must have been to Mrs. Kimball! I swear, Evie, I don't see why we have to take over that boy for the summer just because his mother can't handle him."

Why, indeed! Evie agreed indignantly, and a moment later she went upstairs to put away all the things Matt Jewel was not to find while he was there.

Two

SHE PUT HER MIND TO the task at hand: what to take and what to hide. Opening the chest beneath her window, Evie took out the small patchwork quilt she'd been sewing on since Christmas. It was to be a surprise for Donna Jean's baby, stitched in overlapping petals of yellow and green because they reminded her of spring, of new life about to begin. There was space in one corner to embroider the baby's name.

She put the quilt in the bottom of her suitcase and walked slowly around the room, ducking her head where the roof sloped low, checking her shelves for things Matt Jewel was not to see. There weren't many secrets in her life, she had to conclude. Every time she considered putting something away, she asked herself why Matt would even trouble about it in the first place.

The only things left were her journals—faded blue ledger books, one filled, the other only begun. Just as she delighted in scraps of patterned cloth or bits of colored glass or wood shavings, she loved collecting poems, phrases or possibly even a single word that somehow caught her fancy. "Tintinnabulation" was one. "Lavinia Verna" was another. (She'd found that in the phone book). Sometimes she recorded thoughts of her own.

She sat down and leafed through a few pages of quotes in the first book:

> *Trust thyself; every heart vibrates to that iron string.*
>
> —Emerson

> *I will have no man in my boat who is not afraid of a whale.*
>
> —Captain Starbuck in *Moby Dick*

There were some she had received from her father.

> *The mind is its own place*
> *and in itself*
> *Can make a heaven of hell*
> *a hell of heaven.*
> —John Milton

And then, one of her favorites, a quote from a Blackfoot Indian chief named Crowfoot:

What is life?
It is the breath of a buffalo in wintertime.
It is the little shadow,
   which runs across the grass
   and loses itself in the sunset.

Suddenly she knew that whatever else Matt Jewel might find in her room, she did not want him to read her journals. She could just hear him making some smart-aleck remark. She got up and buried the filled book beneath the remaining blankets in her chest and stuck the unfinished journal in her suitcase.

"Help."

A strangely calm but insistent voice came from one of the lower bedrooms. Like the ring of a telephone, it was repeated again and again at regular intervals.

"Evie, can you tend to Sister Ozzie?" Aunt Ida called. "I've got my hands in the bread dough. Soon as the cartoons is over, she starts that yelling."

Evie went downstairs and into the bedroom in back of the kitchen. A tall, angular woman in a short nightdress was sitting on the edge of the bed, rocking back and forth. Her wrinkled cheeks were heavily rouged, and a jagged line of lipstick cut across her mouth. Like a veil, her white hair hung in wisps about her face and shoulders.

"I want to see Mama," said Sister Ozzie.

"Your mama's not here, but I am. What would you like?"

"I want to go to the bathroom."

"Are you sure?"

"I want to put on my make-up."

It was attention she wanted, then. *An old fool's vanity,* Aunt Ida had said about the cosmetics. *She never wore any all the years she sang in the choir, and why she wants it now that her mind's gone, I don't know.*

Evie took a box from the night stand and handed Ozzie a mirror. The old woman stared intently at her own reflection.

"Who's that?" she asked sharply.

"It's you, Sister Ozzie."

The tall woman frowned.

"Now what you need," Evie told her, "is something to highlight your eyes. Hold real still."

The white-haired lady began to smile. Carefully Evie rubbed a sponge-tipped stick in the blue mascara and smeared it under Sister Ozzie's eyebrows. Even there, the skin was finely wrinkled, like crepe.

"You're going to be so beautiful that men will go absolutely mad," Evie told her. "They'll be pounding on the door day and night."

Sister Ozzie giggled, then scolded, "Well, go on. You always stop."

"The first man will say, 'Sister Ozzie,' " and Evie lowered her voice, " 'I've brung you these here flowers to put on your table.' And you will lift one long finger, and the butler will throw him out. Close your eyes, now."

"What butler?"

"Murphy."

"Oh."

"Then the second man will knock on your door, and he'll say, 'Sister Ozzie, I've brought you some flowers to wear on your dress.' "

The old woman's eyelids fluttered. "And I'll take them, won't I?"

"Nope." Evie smoothed out the spots of rouge that Sister Ozzie had applied herself that morning. "You'll just smile and say, 'No, thank you,' and Murphy will show him out. Because you're waiting for the third man, see. Then *he'll* knock and say, 'Ah, Mademoiselle, here are the most beautiful flowers in all the world to wear in your bea-utiful hair.' "

"I'll take them!" Sister Ozzie cried.

"Of course, you will, and he'll pin them behind your ear, whispering adoringly. . . ."

"Evelyn Hutchins, that is about the silliest thing I ever heard," said a voice from the doorway, but Aunt Ida chuckled as she passed by.

24

Sister Ozzie put one wrinkled hand over Evie's and said, "I certainly do like your stories." And for one brief moment it seemed that the old woman had a grasp on time and place before she let them slip away once more. Would she even remember her, Evie wondered, come September?

There had been a long stretch of time when Evie had not seen her cousin much at all. Before that, when her mother died, Donna Jean had come up from Georgia and made her home with Evie's family for a year. Wilma had just eloped, so Donna Jean was given the twin bed in Rose's room. It was nice having three girls in the house once again. And then Donna Jean married Tom Rawley, and once the wedding was over in the little stucco church, the Rawleys didn't come back to service at all. They never came to visit the Hutchinses. Somehow it was Tom who was blamed.

"It's a sin and a shame," Aunt Ida said of it, yet no one could help liking Tom Rawley, who taught science in the middle school. So they kept their comments to themselves, except that now and then at Sunday dinner, Evie's mother would remember them in prayer.

Yet it was Donna Jean who, quite recently, had helped Evie crystalize what it was she wanted to do with her life. Evie had too many interests, actually. Anything that was pleasing to the eye or touch or ear made her want to be a part of it. To begin with scarcely nothing at all—a lump of clay, a piece of wood, a basket of sewing scraps, a sheet of paper—and create, in turn, a bowl, a carving, a quilt, or a poem—that was what she wanted to do.

But she hadn't really known of a way to put it to use until, quite by accident, she had run into Donna Jean last year at the library, absorbed in a book on stained glass.

"Evie, look at this!" Donna Jean had said, calling her over, bursting, it seemed, to share it with someone. Slowly they had sat turning the pages. There were colored photos of towering stained glass windows in cathedrals and small round windows in farm houses; of lampshades made of intricate patterns of translucent violet, blue, and green; of jewelry boxes and pencil holders, all shimmering like fragments of a shattered rainbow.

When they reached the last page, the afternoon was half over, and they had discovered that despite their nine-year difference in ages, they shared a love of beautiful things, whatever hands like theirs could make. That was the beginning of their seeing one another again, generally on Saturday afternoons.

When the weekly trips to the Rawleys' apartment began, however, they had an unsettling effect back home. To Evie, her family's uneasiness was like a whiff of the ocean: she could sense it long before she could prove it was there.

"Again?" Mother said periodically when Evie asked for the weekly ride over.

And once, in the car beside her father, a basket of yarn on her lap, Evie was hardly surprised when he cleared his throat, hesitated, then asked, "What do you *do* there every Saturday, honey?"

"We take off all our clothes and dance around the table," she told him.

He smiled slowly, not turning his eyes from the road. "Can do a mighty lot of dancing in five hours."

"Ask a silly question. . . ."

"Well, we wonder sometimes. I guess we didn't know you were so taken with quilts."

"It's not just quilts, Dad. You should *see* the things we make! Last Saturday Donna Jean had some wood shavings—big slivers of pine—and we cut them into petal shapes and glued them to dogwood twigs. They are so beautiful you wouldn't believe!" And then she told him: "You know what we're thinking about? Starting a shop. We're saving it all for that."

He glanced at her, wondering, and Evie continued, her words coming out in a rush: "Like Donna Jean says, why should all those rich folks in McLean and Potomac have to drive down to North Carolina to get a handcrafted chair or a quilt or a pitcher? Why can't Branbury become known as a crafts center? We'd drive all over Maryland and get artists to let us sell their things on consignment—pottery and wooden boxes and stuff."

There. It was out. All these months she had not dared mention it for fear the mere sound of the syllables would do away with the dream. For the first time Evie had begun to see how all the assorted threads of her interests might be woven into a single cloth, had felt she had a grip on her life, a direction. She wouldn't just wind up clerking at the five-and-ten because she couldn't make up her mind. She had waited for her father's reaction.

"Well, don't know that you'll ever be able to make a living at it," he had said, "but you'll never find out unless you try."

And she had sunk back against the seat, relieved. "Exactly."

But now as she thought about spending the whole summer with Donna Jean and Tom, as the time to leave was only hours away, a bit of uneasiness seized her. Perhaps it was a mistake, her going.

I'll come back for a day in August when they put up preserves, she thought, and felt better. She would remember to tell Mother that before she left.

Sue called her that evening.
"Is he there yet?"
"Who?"
"That *boy*, Evie!"

"No. Tomorrow sometime. I don't know what you're so excited about."

"Well, it's romantic, that's what. A guy sleeping in your room. . . ."

"Sue! You just said yesterday it was creepy!"

"Well, it's romantic *and* creepy. Every time he crawls in bed he'll think of you."

Evie slid down the wall until she was in a sitting position. "I tell you what. I'll leave your phone number on my pillow."

"Oh, I could never do that—take a boy away from someone."

"Sue, he's not mine! I don't *want* him!"

"What does he look like?"

"I don't know. The last time I saw him we were in fourth grade, and he was short."

"What's so awful about him, anyway?"

Evie tried to put it into words. What was it, exactly, besides the pranks he had pulled in church? Lots of kids pulled pranks.

"One thing I remember," she said, "we were supposed to dramatize Bible scenes for Children's Day, and Matt talked our class into doing the Ark of the Covenant."

"Noah's ark, you mean?"

"No, what the Israelites kept the Commandments in." *Good heavens, didn't the Methodists know anything?* "One of the kids played David, and we had this big chest on poles, and we were carrying it around and banging on cymbals and everything. And then one of the oxen stumbled and the Ark wobbled and Matt—who was Uzzah—put out his hand to steady it, and God killed him."

"What did God do that for?"

"Because he had warned everybody never to touch the Ark. And after Matt fell down and rolled over, he lifted his head and said, 'It's not fair.' I mean, he was always doing things like that."

"Well, it *doesn't* seem fair," said Sue. "But if God told them not to touch it. . . ."

"Anyway, Matt was always bothering me—because Dad was the minister, I suppose. Everytime he opened his mouth, it was something else. He told me once that God had some bears kill little children, and I didn't believe him; so I looked it up in the Bible, and he was right."

"You mean Daniel in the lions' den?"

"No, *bears*, Sue. The ones that came out of the woods and tore into the children making fun of Elisha."

"I never read anything about that in *my* Bible," said Sue.

"Second Kings two: twenty-four," Evie told her. "You sure you want to meet Matt Jewel?"

"Why not? It's going to be a long, slow summer."

After the call, Evie was finishing packing and making room in her bureau for Matt when she was conscious of someone watching from her doorway. She turned to see her father, tall and ungainly, with red-brown skin more like a farmer's than a minister's.

"Came up to have a look at that screen," he said, "where the bugs are getting through."

"Come on in."

He went over to the window and ran one finger along the bottom.

"I probably put the fool screen on upside down," he said and, bending over, squeezed a long ribbon of sealing putty into the crack. "Just got to thinking, standing there in your doorway, that one of these days I'll be watching my girl pack up to get married."

There was a gentleness about him that Evie loved. For a man who got up in the pulpit every Sunday and talked to a hundred and fifty people, he seemed almost shy at times with his family. She smiled at him, even though he didn't see it.

"I'm only going a few miles up the road," she told him.

"Well, I know I've got to lose you some time, but just don't you run off the way Wilma did. I'd always figured on being the preacher at my daughters' weddings. It hurt to know she stood up before someone didn't hardly know her name."

Evie remembered a favorite saying of Aunt Ida's:

When they're small they step on your feet, but when they're grown, they step on your heart.

"It's the last thing on my mind, getting married," she told her father. It wasn't, exactly, but it wasn't first, either.

"Last thing on everybody's mind, it seems, till they meet up with someone, and then it happens so fast they can hardly blink their eyes."

Evie dumped everything from one drawer into another. "Well, if you're so worried about me running off with someone, you oughtn't to go inviting folks here for the summer." She watched him out of the corner of her eye. "I just think I'm going around tomorrow and tell everybody how you got a boy up here sleeping in my room."

Mr. Hutchins raised his head quickly, and they both laughed.

"I wouldn't have hired him if I didn't think he needed it so bad."

Evie's father wiped his hands on his old paint pants and sat down on the chest. "His mother works, and she's afraid he might get in with the wrong crowd over the summer. No jobs in Waldorf to speak of."

"Have you seen him recently? What's he like?"

"Bright. Brighter than his mother. That's the problem, I suppose."

"Well, Aunt Ida sure is unhappy he's coming, and now she's got Rose all stirred up."

A smile flitted across her father's face. "Honey, the only folks your aunt never says a bad word against are the dead, so there's not much future in trying to please her."

They laughed again.

"What we ought to do is marry off Aunt Ida," Evie suggested mischievously.

"Wouldn't change a thing. People keep looking for something else to turn things around for them. And all the time they've got the power to be happy or sad right inside themselves."

Evie watched her father get up, his head bent forward so as not to bump the low ceiling, the soft wrinkles from thousands of summer days on his face, and she knew that there was no way in the world she would ever hurt this man.

Three

ON SUNDAY MORNINGS, the moment Evie liked best was leaving the dank musty odor of the basement Bible-school rooms for the unique aromas of the sanctuary—the carpeting, the ink of the hymn books, the aging wood pews.   Mrs. Anderson was playing the piano as she had for twenty years, her head bent forward sharply as she followed the music through thick-lensed glasses. Rose and Mrs. Hutchins were seated in a pew on the right, and Evie slipped in beside them, her blue dress mingling with the folds of Rose's green print.

A young man with curly hair started to sit down in the row in front, then turned and shook hands with Mrs. Hutchins. But it was Rose who had caught his eye; when he took her hand next, he merely nodded to Evie and kept holding Rose's fingers in his.

"A few of us are taking my boat out on the river Saturday," he told her. "We'd love to have you come."

"Oh, Rose, that would be fun!" Mrs. Hutchins encouraged.

Evie's sister slowly disentangled her fingers from the sturdy hand. "Saturday's a bad day for me. I have to be at the drive-in window till noon."

"We'll wait, if you can make it."

"Oh, I just don't think I'd better."

The young man's smile seemed to shrink, but his voice took on a new softness. "You name the day, and we'll set another time," he told her.

Rose only laughed and spread her hands out flat on her lap, smoothing her dress, and finally the man with the curly hair gave up.

Evie glanced at her sister. Time and again Rose turned down offers, as though she couldn't believe she was wanted, as though she were waiting for only one man in her life, and until he came, she wouldn't date anyone. How would she ever know if she never went out?

"Same old silly people, laughing and getting wet, and me not even knowing how to swim," Rose murmured, as if to fend off her questions.

Mrs. Anderson was playing Bach. Down at the Methodist Church they played hymns on the organ for the opening music, and over at the Baptist, the organist mixed them into a medley, "Lead Kindly

Light" becoming "Oh, Jesus I Have Promised" without any break in between. But here in Pa Hutchins' church, where there was only an upright piano, a woman with a love of the baroque played Bach every Sunday as though to defy the circumstances that had kept her in Branbury. It was a matter of considerable pride.

The music was very busy, hardly pausing for a minute, with notes chasing each other in every direction. It reminded Evie of an elaborately carved doorframe that she and Donna Jean had seen once, scrolls and flowers and birds and trumpets all twisting together, curving back upon themselves and then whirling on in endless variation.

The choir came in through a side door behind the pulpit and sat in folding chairs beyond the piano. At that moment Evie was conscious of two late arrivals entering her pew and glanced over.

A small woman in a navy blue hat and a box-shaped boy about Evie's age were moving sideways along the row. No sooner had the woman sat down than Mrs. Hutchins leaned over, across her daughters' laps, and clasped the woman's hand warmly:

"Sister Jewel!"

"Sister Hutchins!"

Evie rigidly pressed herself against the back of the pew. The blood seemed to rush to her cheeks, and she could not bring herself to look at Matt. Stupidly, all she could think of was the sound of her own crying when he had locked her in the church broom closet. Anger washed over her. She was not prepared for this—had thought perhaps Matt would arrive after she had left for Donna Jean's.

As the congregation rose for the first hymn, however, her persistent refusal to acknowledge him seemed awkward and childish. So when she passed Matt and his mother a hymnal, she forced herself to look Matt straight in the eyes—brown eyes, somewhat close together beneath a lighter shock of hair. He glanced away.

It was a favorite hymn, and the people sang lustily, their voices sliding up to the high notes and down to the low, hitting all the steps in between:

"Rescue the perishing, care for the dying,
Snatch them in pity from sin and the grave;
Weep o'er the erring one,
Lift up the fallen,
Tell them of Jesus the mighty to save."

Matt was not singing. Evie could see his thumb on the hymn book—a large thumb with a broad flat nail—and beyond it the gray weave of his jacket cuff. The hymn went on for four verses. Mrs. Anderson banged out the beat, vigorously nodding her head in time with the music, but the congregation would not be hurried and dawdled a half-measure behind:

"Tho' they are slighting Him,
Still He is waiting,
Waiting the penitent child to receive;
Plead with them earnestly,
Plead with them gently,
He will forgive if they only believe."

Finally, as the hymn books closed, Evie made one more effort to smile at Matt. But he stared back at her with sardonic aloofness from a face that was broad, like his thumb.

Smart-alecky, just like his mother said, Evie thought and, when she sat, turned her back on him.

As the service continued, however, she could not help noticing his feet. The black scuffed shoes went under the pew during the anthem, then stretched out under the seat in front during the Scripture. One ankle crossed over a knee during Mr. Hutchins' morning prayer, and at the words, ". . . forever and ever, world without end," the foot came down again, the legs spread out, and the feet rested, toes up, on the heels.

There was the offertory, then a solo, and finally Mr. Hutchins stood up to begin the sermon. Here in the pulpit he talked louder, more boldly. He used his hands to dramatize, his fist for emphasis, and there was a lilt and rhythm to his voice that Evie loved. The topic on this particular Sunday was penitence, as she might have guessed, for he often chose the first hymn of the morning to reinforce his theme.

"Wherever we go," he was saying, "God is there and He is patient. However long it may take us to give our hearts to Him, He will wait. No matter how many times we fall, He is ready to accept us again and forgive. His mercy is everlasting and His truth endureth forever." Then he told the story of the prodigal son.

Evie had heard better sermons by her father. Yet this one was certainly better than the one by the short little preacher from Parkville last month who stood on his toes, the choir had said, through the whole sermon. The preacher from Parkville seemed to go on and on without any subject at all, touching upon sin and grace and glory, his voice falling at the end of each sentence until you could hardly hear him. Still, Evie wished that on this particular Sunday, with Matt Jewel in the pew, her father had talked of something else—something Matt couldn't laugh at. And when the sermon reached twenty-five minutes and still showed no signs of concluding, she sat with her head down, hoping somehow that her father would get the cue.

A fly landed on Rose's knee—a large fly with green-gold wings—and she waved it away. It alighted next on the white curls of a woman in front and walked about unnoticed for a moment before floating down to Evie's arm, tickling with its spindly feet. Evie brushed it off, and this time the fly landed on the right hand of Matt Jewel.

Ready for a distraction, Evie turned and watched. Matt did not shoo it away. The fly sat with its glistening wings spread out, rubbing its back legs together. Then it walked a pace or two, stopped, and began rubbing again.

Matt's left hand rose slowly off the seat, higher, higher, his fingers cupped together. Suddenly . . . *whup!* The horsefly buzzed frantically in its prison. Matt's mother nudged him and shook her head.

"Honestly!" Rose whispered under her breath.

Mercifully, Evie thought, the sermon was ending. As soon as the choir had sung the benediction and the postlude began, Mrs. Hutchins and Mrs. Jewel turned toward each other, squeezing past Rose and Evie, and embraced.

"How good to see you again!" Mother said, and included Matt in her welcome. "So this is our son for the summer. I don't think I would have recognized you, Matt." She put out her hand, and Matt shook it.

"Do you remember Rose?" she asked.

Rose put out her hand coldly, and Matt took it also.

"And Evie, of course, our youngest."

Matt's hand was extended toward her, and because he appeared to be smiling, Evie put out her own. Instead of shaking it, however, he merely turned it over and, with his left hand, deposited the still-live fly on her palm.

She drew back sharply as the fly buzzed off. Matt was laughing.

"Matthew!" said his mother in exasperation.

"Very funny," said Evie icily. The same old Matt!

He shrugged. "I thought you might appreciate it. It was bothering everybody."

"It wasn't the fly that was bothering," Evie retorted.

Mrs. Jewel turned helplessly toward Mrs. Hutchins. "Not enough to do, that's his problem."

Evie's mother laughed. "Well, we'll solve that in a hurry. We're really pleased you can help us out this summer, Matt. It will be nice having a young man about the place."

And then they were all moving slowly up the aisle, through the lobby where Mr. Hutchins was shaking hands with his parishioners, and on outside.

Matt's mother, of course, was invited to the Hutchinses' place after church. There was always someone extra on Sunday. On this day, because of the unusual warm spell, the meal would be eaten outdoors.

Mrs. Jewel, still wearing her navy blue hat, slipped one of Mother's aprons over her jersey dress.

"How can I help?" she insisted. "You just put me to work, now—God didn't make me useless."

"Why, Sister Jewel, we didn't invite you here to mess up that dress," Aunt Ida bantered good-naturedly.

Evie took a stack of plates to the folding table on the porch. Through the screen, she could see out over the north pasture where her father was showing Matt around—the rundown barn, the empty goat shed. She could hardly bear to look at the boy. He brought back too many feelings of ridicule. She had never been comfortable around him—*never.* This whole exchange was more embarrassing still—simply a ceremony, the ritual filling of a vacant room. What would her parents do when both she and Rose were gone? She envisioned the place overrun with people like Matt: the Hutchinses' Home for Incorrigibles.

Self-consciously she watched when everyone crowded onto the narrow back porch to fill their plates, how ridiculous it all was: the absurdity of using chipped everyday cups and saucers because it was too difficult to get to the cut-glass dinnerware in the dining room; the necessity of using a rickety folding table covered with oil cloth because the big oak table beside Mr. Schmidt's bed had long since become a repository for folded towels and sheets.

She hung back while the Jewels went first in line. Mrs. Hutchins presided from the doorway between the kitchen and porch, asking them all to pause a moment while Father asked the blessing, then warmly calling their attention to the buttered rolls, the barbequed beans, and the chicken, crisp-fried, on the platter.

They moved out to the beech tree where Murphy was industriously setting up folding chairs, and Evie sat down on a log edging the rose garden, slightly behind the others. Even there, she discovered, she could not escape Matt's eyes, and she tried sitting sideways, staring off at the walnut grove behind the house. In a few more hours Donna Jean's husband would come to drive her to the home they had bought, and she would be rid of Matt forever.

There was the usual buzz of Sunday chatter—compliments over the food, the merits of the sermon, the number in attendance. . . . She remembered when Matt had removed the first two numbers from the little signboard near the front of the sanctuary so that the number in attendance for the previous Sunday read "0" instead of "130." It had got to the place where anytime something went wrong at church, Matt Jewel was the first person blamed.

Murphy was running back and forth between the beech tree and the kitchen, doing errands. He brought the butter but had forgotten the ice water. Embarrassed, he went back.

"And bring Sister Ozzie an orange," Aunt Ida called after him, frowning at the elderly woman who was talking softly, animatedly, to the beans on her plate. She turned to Mrs. Jewel. "My, we have a time of it, though, getting Ozzie to eat. Nothing seems to taste good to her these days."

Rose nodded: "Milk's sour, she says; meat's rotten. Only thing she'll eat for sure is oranges."

"Then thank the Lord He left her something she could still enjoy," said Mother.

Evie glanced over at Matt, thinking he might be distracted, but he was still watching her. She tried to keep her eyes steady this time and not let him scare her off; but after a moment or two, she turned away and felt her face flush.

She tried thinking of him as a person to be pitied. He was, after all, being raised fatherless. Mr. Jewel had deserted his family when Matt was in first grade, and—the story went—Matt had been a holy terror ever since.

"You can leave off the 'holy,' " Aunt Ida said of him once. "That boy is cut from a different cloth, that's all there is to it."

No, Evie thought. There was more to it than that. It wasn't just his pranks or the fact that he was fatherless. It was that Matt had a genius, it seemed, for making her feel disturbed, uncertain; for raising questions that couldn't be answered.

When the hired man returned again, he had the ice water but not the orange.

"Murphy, I declare!" said Rose.

Murphy glanced about him in confusion and opened his mouth, but nothing came out.

44

"I'll get it," Evie said. "Mr. Schmidt needs checking anyway. Sit down, Murphy. You haven't had a bite yet."

She gathered up her own dishes. The hired man turned his chair away from the others and began eating glumly.

"Now don't you sit there and sulk," Aunt Ida said to him. "Nobody did you no harm, Murphy."

"Let him be," said Mr. Hutchins, and the conversation turned to other things.

Evie wished she could speed up the clock and somehow be standing at the end of the drive so Tom Rawley wouldn't even have to turn in. She wished she could just set her tray in the kitchen, go upstairs for her suitcase, and not have to go back out to the others. It was not the feeling she'd wanted to have when she left home for the summer.

Mr. Schmidt was listening to the radio beside his bed, seemingly content. He had not walked since his stroke, but enjoyed having music about him. Quietly Evie backed out of the room and through the pantry again. When she stepped into the kitchen, she found herself face to face with Matt.

"Where should I put these?" he asked, holding his plate and cup.

"Anywhere," she told him. "The sink, I guess."

He put the dishes down, but did not leave.

"Listen," he said. "I'm sorry about the fly. Sometimes I just do dumb things."

Evie studied him. She could not tell if it was a real apology or just another sarcastic jeer, a fake humility to point up how super-sensitive she had been.

She managed a small smile. "It was dumb, all right."

"I know. Really stupid. I just do things without thinking." He stood there by the refrigerator, nervously cracking his knuckles, and Evie decided that maybe it was for real, a side to Matt she'd never seen. "Mom said you're going away for the summer," he added.

"Just down the road a few miles to stay with my cousin."

"I kick you out or something?"

"No, I'd already planned to go. Donna Jean's expecting a baby."

"Oh. Well, I mean, if I had, I could go back home. It's not like I really need this job, and this isn't what you'd call a fun place."

Evie stared at him. He hadn't changed at all.

"Don't do me any favors," she said, and abruptly left the room.

About three-thirty, Tom Rawley's old green Dodge came winding up the drive. Mrs. Jewel had already taken her leave, and Donna Jean's husband was a welcome replacement.

"Hi, Ma Hutchins," he said, hugging Evie's

mother. "How you doing, Aunt Ida?" Rose was already retreating toward the house, so Tom shook Father's hand next, made a special point of shaking Murphy's also, then turned to Matt.

"This is the boy we've hired for the summer," Mr. Hutchins told him. "Matt, this is Tom Rawley. Evie's staying with him and his wife."

"Nice to meet you," said Matt.

"You should have brought that girl here for dinner, Tom," Aunt Ida scolded, ignoring the fact that Donna Jean hadn't been back to the house since she married. "You *know* you're invited, and she needs her nourishment."

"Donna Jean says she's too uncomfortable to go anywhere," Tom explained genially. "Says it's even too much trouble to put on her shoes."

"Well, don't you suppose we haven't had us bare feet around here before?"

"Anyway, she's resting. Thinks if she just lies around and wishes, the baby will get here all the sooner."

Mother laughed. "That child will come when it's good and ready."

"I'll go get your suitcase, Evie," her father said, and Evie followed him upstairs to make one last check of her room. She discovered that Matt had already stacked his things in one corner, and suddenly the room didn't seem hers anymore.

"I've got everything," she said, and went back out

in the hall. She had wanted to say something warm and special to her father before she left, something humorous and corny perhaps, such as, "Think of it this way, Dad; you're losing a daughter but gaining a son." On the stairs going down, however, he told her:

"Remember this, honey; you're a witness for Jesus Christ to Tom and Donna Jean. 'Let your light so shine. . . .' It may be you're going there for a purpose."

And because Evie could think of no reply, she said nothing at all.

Matt stood off to himself, hands in his pockets, as she kissed the others and got in the car. And then the Dodge was turning around by the beech tree, heading for the road.

Four

EVERY SO OFTEN there was a break in the trees, some cleared land, and a small frame house would come into view next to a tobacco field. *Turkey Shoot*, a sign read. *Every Sunday. Eleven till five.* And further still, *Calvary Baptist Church Welcomes You.* Past the firehouse and the one-room post office, no larger itself than a two-cent stamp.

"Not going to get homesick, are you?" Tom asked.

"I've never been away long enough to know," Evie told him. "Not much to get homesick for, with Matt Jewel in my room."

"He seems likable enough." Tom gave her a sidelong glance beneath the red eyebrows that matched his flaming orange hair. He was as fair-skinned as Mr. Hutchins was brown, and his nose and cheeks showed sunburn from a weekend's work in the yard.

"Huh," Evie said, turning toward the window again, wishing they were going further, a day's distance, at least.

She had never been away from home overnight— out of Charles County, that is—except for a trip to Baltimore to visit Wilma. She wondered what it would be like to live there, in a row of hooked-together houses, each with its own marble stoop— where you could hardly walk across the street without getting run over. Here, people cared. They remembered your birthday before you thought of it yourself. In Baltimore, the neighbors didn't even know your name.

Tom turned onto the highway at the Texaco station, passed Hollander's Grocery, and then, a mile down, just beyond the low-lying cemetery, turned again onto a dirt lane.

At this very spot, Evie was thinking, there would soon be a sign saying *The Cousins*. Or perhaps it would read, *The Cousins: Quilt and Craft Shop;* she and Donna Jean could never decide which. And perhaps there would be an arrow at the bottom of the sign pointing the way. The trees closed in over them, a canopy of green. Two-hundred yards on, the lane came to an end, and they were there.

The old Gettinger house, now the Rawleys', looked like an aging woman who had put on a few touches for company. Geraniums spilled out of a milk can at the top of the steps and again in a bucket near the door. Large sheets of dyed Indian cotton, with intricate purple and turquoise designs, hung at the two front windows, and at each, the curtains had been pulled to one side in a graceful curve, like an old woman's hair, parted in the middle.

And then the front door was opening, and there stood Donna Jean, her belly big as Christmas, arms outstretched. Evie leaned in over the bulging abdomen and hugged her.

"I keep telling her, if the baby gets any bigger, she won't be able to sit up to the table." Tom smiled, hoisting Evie's suitcase onto the porch.

"It'll be a good thing, too!" Donna Jean said. "*Look* at me, Evie! I never cared much for food before, and now I eat everything in sight. Come on. I want you to see the nursery. We just finished it yesterday. You'll be sleeping there this summer. We want to keep the baby in our room for the first few months, anyway."

Evie followed her cousin upstairs. Donna Jean was twenty-five, a year older than Rose, but looked younger because she was small—a light-boned girl with hair like Evie's, which she heaped on top of her head with a tortoise-shell comb. Her skin was covered with thousands of freckles, and her green eyes were always crinkled with some unspoken merriment. A flower child, Mother called her.

They walked down the creaky hall, past other bedrooms, empty of furniture, the walls untouched and peeling. At the end, however, sun beamed in on a soft yellow room. The long, narrow windows reached almost from ceiling to floor, and along one wall, rows of pear boxes had been nailed together and painted to form a toy cupboard.

"Donna Jean, it's perfect!" Evie breathed, thinking at once how well the quilt she had made would match.

Donna Jean broke into a pleased smile. "Hours! We've spent hours on this room, sanding and varnishing and painting. The baby's not even here yet, and already it's enough work for two!" She stood very still suddenly, then placed Evie's hand on her abdomen. "Feel."

There, beneath the sundress, a lumpy knob moved slowly about, and Evie imagined a baby's knee turning slightly in its sleep.

Donna Jean grinned. "Put your things away and come down in the kitchen. Seems like a month since I saw you."

Tom was sitting at the table, shirt sleeves rolled up. It didn't seem right that there should be such a luxury of quiet—no calls from adjoining rooms, no bustle by the sink, no instructions given followed up by reminders. . . . Evie was conscious not so much of the furnishings as she was of the places where there weren't any—of wide-open rectangles and circles of space, uncluttered by stepstools and medicine bottles and Aunt Ida's salt and pepper collection.

Over frosty jelly glasses of mint tea, they talked about their plans for the next few weeks, contingent, of course, on when the baby came.

"Well, I just hope you're home when it happens," Evie said to Tom. "Please make it an evening or weekend, Donna Jean, or I'll be scared silly."

"Don't worry. We'll have plenty of warning. I've taped the doctor's number above the phone in case you need it."

"Should I call Mother first?"

It seemed to Evie a perfectly acceptable question. When women had their babies at home in Branbury, it was usually Mrs. Hutchins who delivered them. Yet the question seemed to evoke an awkward moment, and Evie caught a quickly exchanged glance between Donna Jean and Tom.

"No, just call the doctor," Donna Jean said. "We've decided to have him do the delivery."

And then the talk shifted to Tom—where he might be reached at summer school—and Evie kept all further questions to herself.

When she woke on Monday, the sun cut twin shafts of light through the uncurtained windows, half-blinding her. Evie dressed quickly.

In the kitchen doorway she stopped, for the table was a wild bouquet of color—of green gingham, blue-checked calico, orange-flowered muslin, and purple broadcloth.

Donna Jean's head emerged from somewhere behind it, and she said, "As soon as Tom is off in the mornings, I clean the table and start my cuttings. Look."

She held up a long skirt made entirely of patches. "I finished this one last week, and I'm starting another like it. I want to have several done when our shop opens."

"It's lovely!"

"But what a mess, huh? It takes an hour some mornings just to make sense of it." Evie's cousin nodded toward the oven. "I just stuck some french toast in there to warm. Come and see what Tom did to our shop this morning. He got up early and hooked on the shelves before he left."

They stood in the large study, soon to be their shop. Somehow the long unpainted shelves, rows and rows of them, made it look official.

"Oh, Donna!" Evie gasped.

"Isn't it exciting!" Donna Jean breathed. "You know, as soon as we saw this house, it was like love at first sight. Just what I wanted, and right off the highway, too. People would say, 'But hardly anybody drives through Branbury.' And we'd answer, 'Don't worry; they will.' "

There was a strange, squeaking, scraping noise outside, and Evie went to the window.

"What is it?" asked Donna Jean.

"Oh, lordy, it's *him*."

"Who?"

"Matt Jewel. He's riding the old bike that Murphy keeps around the place."

"Well, invite him in."

Donna Jean went back to the kitchen and Evie waited reluctantly at the front screen. Matt did not seem especially pleased about coming, either. He leaned his bike against a tree and slipped off the cloth bag that hung from the handlebars.

"Your mother said you forgot to bring these with you yesterday, and she wanted your cousin to have them," he said, coming up on the porch. "Jellies, I think."

"We weren't about to starve," Evie said dryly.

"It wasn't *my* idea." He wiped the perspiration off his forehead, his shirt wet from the ride. "Jars kept bouncing against my knee. A miracle they're not broken."

Evie promised herself she'd be civil. "You want to come in, get a drink of water or something?"

He followed her back to the kitchen where Donna Jean was sorting patchwork again.

"Donna Jean, this is Matt Jewel," Evie said, and let the introduction drop.

"Hi, Matt." Donna Jean gave the same smile to saint and sinner alike. "Oh, blackberry jelly! Tell Mrs. Hutchins I really appreciate it! Like some mint tea? Evie, see if there's any left from last night. In fact. . . ." She looked hopelessly around the table. "Why don't you put your french toast on a tray and take it out on the porch with his tea? There's just no place here to eat."

Evie tried to send a message through her eyes, but Donna Jean had turned away.

They sat on the steps, at opposite ends. For a while there was no sound but the clink of Evie's knife and fork against her plate.

"You just get up or something?" Matt asked, watching. "Or is that your lunch?"

"Yes, I just got up, and no, it's not my lunch," Evie retorted.

"I only asked." He slowly drank the cold tea and looked out over the yard. "Jeez, I thought I'd never find this place. Your mother said turn right at the cemetery, she didn't say before or after. I got all the way down the other road before I realized she probably meant the road after."

Evie smiled a little. "So how was your first morning back at the house?"

He shrugged. "It's hardly even started yet. I was supposed to help Murphy move some logs when your mother asked me to ride over here." He shook his head disgustedly. "When your dad offered me a job this summer, I remembered your place as a big farm. You know—horses, hay, driving a tractor. . . . I forgot it's just a puny little piece of land with some old beat-up buildings and a house full of—" He stopped, checking himself.

Evie stared at him with awed indignation. "Well, why don't you just quit, then? Nobody's begging you to stay that I can see."

"Home's worse," was all he said. He took one more long drink of tea and set the glass on the porch.

Evie went on tensely cutting her toast, then picked up the syrup and poured too much. "Seems to me, with jobs hard to find the way they are, that a person would be grateful."

"I didn't say I wasn't grateful. I just said it wasn't what I was expecting."

"Well, maybe *life* isn't what you expected, Matt! Things aren't always going to be just like you want them. Life is just a string of chances, Aunt Ida always said, and you've got to take your chances like everybody else."

He leaned back against the post, studying her. "Boy, you sure do sound like the old girl when you get cranked up."

"If she yelled at you, you probably deserved it."

"It wasn't me she was yelling at, it was Murphy. He left a shovel on the driveway, and your father backed over it last night. You'd think it was a body Murphy had left out there, the way your aunt carried on."

"She's excitable sometimes, but not Mother."

"That's for sure. Patient angel of mercy, your mother."

Evie quickly gathered up her dishes. "Well, I've got things to do. If you want to sit out here, you can."

"You know what you're sore about? You're still mad about me locking you in the broom closet."

Evie could feel her face start to burn. "Huh! Hardly even remembered it."

Matt smiled, picked up his glass, and followed her back to the kitchen.

"Thanks for the tea," he said to Donna Jean, as Evie stood stiffly by the window.

"Sure. Come by for lunch sometime, Matt. We can use the company."

"He's awful!" Evie said furiously, watching him ride away. "If he comes for lunch, I'm eating in my room."

"Why on earth?"

It was too embarrassing to talk about. "I used to know him when he lived in Branbury," Evie said. "I couldn't stand him then, and I can stand him less now."

"Finish your breakfast," Donna Jean told her, glancing at her half-eaten toast. "The world is full of worse than him."

A storm blew in that evening. The sky turned gray about five o'clock, and by six, dark masses of clouds rolled one over another as the wind picked up. The yellow cat that sat outside on the window ledge, a young stray, now stood at the back door and meowed piteously, and Tom finally let it in. It skittered under the table, ears laid back, and crouched, its eyes glowing.

After each bolt of lightning, the thunder seemed instantaneous. Donna Jean and Evie sat over the remains of supper as Tom went about from room to room checking windows.

"I'll bet that roof leaks again," Donna Jean said, hugging herself and shivering. "Last time, water came down the wall in the middle bedroom." She sat listening for Tom's footsteps overhead. "I always think of Rose when it storms. She was deathly afraid of lightning. Is she still that way?"

"A little."

"That year I stayed with you, when I slept in her room, she would think up all kinds of excuses to go downstairs during a storm. And she'd stay there till it was over."

Evie smiled. "How old was I then? Ten, I guess. It seems a long time ago."

"It was right after Wilma married—right after my mother died. Rose said I was like a sister to her. She couldn't bear looking at Wilma's empty bed." Donna Jean paused. "How *is* Rose?"

"The same as always."

"Does she get out much? Go places?"

"Not really. She's asked, but she doesn't go."

"I wonder if she's ever forgiven me."

Why did she feel suddenly as though she had her hand on the knob of a hidden door? Evie wondered. Why did she sense that if she asked the next question, she would find out something she had never been meant to know? She asked: "For what?"

Donna Jean looked at her curiously, surprised. "For taking Tom," she said, and then stopped as his footsteps sounded on the stairs.

Evie sat without moving, her breath caught in her throat.

"It's coming down that wall again," Tom said wearily. "Wallpaper's puffing out like a balloon. Can't tell where it's getting in."

Donna Jean avoided Evie's questioning eyes. "We'd better go mop up then," she said, and they all trooped upstairs with buckets and towels, and stayed until the thunder receded, like a truck rumbling away in the distance. Evie moved mechanically, saying nothing, feeling puzzled and hurt and, worst of all, disloyal to Rose for having come.

She lay on her bed that night as a light rain continued to fall. Her mind picked at old memories, sorting them out, discarding some, keeping others. The uneasiness she had sensed in her own family seemed to have rolled itself into a ball and come to rest on her stomach. They had all known something she had not, and there was anger along with her confusion. She was tired of her role as the youngest.

There was a light tap on her door, and Donna Jean came in with Tom's robe about her shoulders.

"You awake, Evie?" she whispered.

"Yes."

"I thought you might like some company."

Without answering, Evie moved over and Donna Jean lowered herself down on the trundle bed, leaning back and resting on her hands.

"Oof!" she said. "This kid better come soon. I sure am ready."

"It's waiting for the full moon," Evie suggested. "That's what Mother always said. Has something to do with tides."

"Maybe so." Donna Jean sat silently for a few moments, then said, "I didn't want to leave things dangling—what I said about Rose and Tom. I thought you knew."

"Well, I don't." There was resentment in Evie's voice.

Donna Jean took a breath, held it, then let it out again slowly. "Tom and Rose used to date some in high school. It wasn't a steady thing. He was a senior, she was a junior, and there was a certain crowd that got together every so often. Somehow it was always Tom and Rose who were paired up."

There did seem a time, Evie remembered, when she had seen Tom Rawley before, coming in and out of the house. But in a small town like Branbury, almost everyone had been to the Hutchinses' place at one time or another.

"Well, Tom graduated and the crowd broke up, and he and Rose just drifted apart, the way people do. But Rose evidently missed him a lot, more than he missed her. Tom's family moved to Michigan, but he stayed here to attend the community college, and after Rose graduated, she took a job at the bank. Then I came to live with you and started taking courses at the college."

Even in the darkness, Evie could sense Donna Jean's hesitation.

"I met Tom one day in the cafeteria. I told him about myself, where I was living, and he mentioned that he knew the Hutchins girls. That was all. It was never a big deal with him about Rose, so he didn't think to add anything else. He told me later that he figured Rose had more dates than she could handle."

"And you didn't tell Rose that you were going with Tom?"

"No, because I really wasn't—not yet. It never occurred to me to say anything at all. And then one Saturday Tom got it in his head to drive over."

She shifted about on the bed and rested one hand on her abdomen. "I was upstairs changing the sheets. I heard a car come up your drive, and there was Tom, parking under the beech tree. I ducked in the bathroom to clean up, knowing the others would entertain him till I came down. And then. . . ."

In the pale light of the room, Evie could make out no freckles at all—just an oval face with hollows for eyes. She tried to imagine herself in Donna Jean's place, with a boyfriend parked under the beech tree.

"There are times, Evie, when you just know what happened as surely as if you had seen it all yourself. I stood in the doorway looking at Rose, the way she was sitting there on the arm of the sofa beside Tom, her face flushed, eyes sparkling—just the way she had her ankles crossed, even!—and I knew she thought he'd come for her. Your parents were laughing and talking like it was a big welcome-home party.

"Then Tom saw me and smiled, and in that minute it was as though I had set fire to the house, destroyed it all, hacked it down. Rose stared at me and then at Tom, and her face went gray, like an old pillowcase. Worst of all, everybody went on smiling, talking, acting like it was all right, and I could just see that it wasn't. Your father finally excused himself, and your mother sat down by Rose—as if to protect her—and then Tom asked me if I wanted to go for a drive, and we left. I never felt so strange in my life—awful for Rose, wild for Tom. And yet—I felt angry at your family for presuming too much, for taking the edge off my joy. Oh, it's so irrational. Love always is."

"What happened then?"

"We went for our drive, got a sandwich, and talked and talked. I hate to admit it, but I finally forgot all about Rose till we drove home again. When I went upstairs, she was in bed, her back to me. I tried to talk to her, but she pretended she was asleep. The pity of it is, we never did talk. Rose avoided me, never gave me a chance. I even wrote her a letter once and left it on her dresser. I found the envelope later, unopened."

Evie could picture it all—the excitement, the disappointment, the joy, the pain. . . . She suddenly felt very close to Donna Jean.

"Did you ever tell Mother?"

"Yes. She was very understanding—said that Rose would grow used to it in time, would find someone else. But Rose never did. I came and went and tried to spend as little time at your house as possible. Whenever Tom came to get me, I'd be waiting for him outside so that Rose wouldn't be uncomfortable. When we married, you can't imagine the relief I felt in getting away."

It was as though Evie were standing out on the road looking at her house, her family, from a completely different angle. Yet she too had felt a kind of relief when Tom came to drive her away, and it wasn't entirely because of Matt Jewel.

"Well, it wasn't your fault, Donna Jean."

"Of course not. But it didn't make me feel any better around Rose, or her around me. I loved your parents, Evie, and Aunt Ida too, bless her cranky old soul. But I've just never felt easy going back there and I think up all kinds of excuses not to."

"I'm glad you feel comfortable around me," Evie said at last.

Donna Jean leaned down impulsively and hugged her. And then the baby kicked—so hard that Evie felt it. They laughed, and the laughter, like the rain outside, seemed to cleanse the air around them. For the time being, anyway.

Five

THE WEEK MOVED in slow motion, as though mimicking Donna Jean. Mornings were spent in the kitchen, afternoons on the porch, and an hour before Tom came home, Donna Jean would lie on the sofa with her feet up.

There was a tenderness about this household that Evie enjoyed. She liked Tom's homecomings especially, when he always brought a present for Donna Jean, something to make her laugh. One day it would be a bunch of dandelions, wilted by the time they reached the door; sometimes a *Mad* magazine, or a packet of sugar from the school cafeteria. There was the afternoon he arrived with three plastic straws, and they all sat around the porch after supper blowing kernels of unpopped corn at each other, shrieking like banshees when they were hit. Evie could not even imagine her family doing something that was just plain silly and fun.

Once, tired of her heaviness, Donna Jean had cried, her nose pink and puffy. "I'm going to stay this way forever," she had wept. "I'll be as big as an elephant and have varicose veins and stretch marks and swollen feet. . . ." And then they had laughed together, even as she was crying, and Tom held her, rubbing the small of her back.

There was more touching in this house than there was back home. Not that the Hutchinses weren't affectionate. But here Donna Jean and Tom seemed to reach out to each other naturally and often. It was all so spontaneous that Evie never felt like an intruder.

Still, living with the Rawleys had meant some adjustments. Not only were there open spaces in the sparsely furnished rooms, there were spaces in sound as well—times when there were no voices at all, when Evie and Tom and Donna Jean would pause in their after-dinner chatter and sit idly, allowing thoughts to go in and out of their heads at will. For a day or two, this had unnerved her, these lapses in conversation, these pieces of silence. But they all seemed to fit in with the rose there in a vase, the earthenware crocks on the counter, the handmade broom in one corner, and the bare oak floors. They belonged.

Study to be quiet, and to do your own business, and to work with your own hands, came a verse to her from Thessalonians. She would write it in her journal.

Hollander's Grocery was a gray two-room store that had been on the highway at least as long as the Texaco. Empty Pepsi crates were stacked on one side of the porch and bags of fertilizer on the other. A soft drink machine was crammed between the door and the window.

The walk was longer than Evie had anticipated. It was only the tenth of June, but the air was hot, the heat clinging. Despite the cut-offs and tee shirt, she could feel the perspiration running down the back of her legs, and a blister was forming beneath one sandal strap.

Crossing the gravel parking lot in front of the store, she heard the sound of drumming from inside—a faint, tinny roll that gradually turned into a syncopated beat. It sounded as though someone were tapping out a rhythm on a Crisco can.

She peered through the screen, then opened it softly and stepped under the long strip of fly paper hanging from the ceiling. Yes, someone was standing behind the counter, tapping out a rhythm on a Crisco can—also on a potato chip box, a Hi-C container, and an aluminum pie pan suspended from a hook under a shelf.

It certainly wasn't Mr. Hollander. The boy was blond, far more blond than Evie, rather tall and thin. Skinny, even. Though his face was turned away from her, she could see the concentrated set of his lips as his hands fluttered and shook over the makeshift drum set.

She waited, then moved slowly around the edge of his vision.

The playing stopped abruptly, and a faint blush spread up the boy's neck like mercury in a thermometer.

"Sorry, I didn't hear you come in."

She smiled. "If I'd walked through the window glass, you wouldn't have heard me either."

He smiled too and nodded toward the arrangement of cans, thrusting his drumsticks in a hip pocket. "Just practicing. It's my lunch break so I figure I can mess around a little. Can I help you?"

"You work here?"

"Yeah. For the summer."

"Right now I just want an orange soda. It's scorching out there, and I've got a blister." She rested one foot on her knee and examined it.

"Want a Band-aid?"

"Yes, if you have one."

The boy went into the back room and returned. He carefully peeled off the tabs of the bandage and knelt down, applying it gently over her heel. His hair was so blond that it was almost white, and the whiteness of his eyebrows gave the appearance of no brows at all. Still, there was a fine shadow of a mustache above his lip.

"There." He stood up. "Feel okay?"

"Fine, thanks."

He went behind the counter to get change for her dollar and followed her out to the porch. "Live around here?"

"Yes, but I'm staying with my cousin this summer. She's expecting a baby any day." Evie put a coin in the slot, watching him, trying to remember him from school. "Are you a senior?"

"I was. Just graduated this week. I live back in Silver Spring with my mother."

"What are you doing over here?"

"I stay with my dad summers. He was transferred to Naval Ordnance this year." The boy hoisted himself up on the bags of fertilizer and watched her.

Evie sat on the steps and slowly sipped her soda. "Do you like it here?" she asked.

"Pretty much. I've just been around a couple days. Always before, see, Dad took an apartment, but this time he rented a house so I could bring my drums along."

"Do you play in a band?"

"I used to. Now I get together back home with some guys and we jam. Write our own songs and everything. We made a couple tapes and left one with a disc jockey, but I don't know if he ever listened to it or not." He smiled. "I'm Chris Lundgren, by the way."

"Evie Hutchins."

"Pleased to meet you."

70

They laughed.

The back door slammed, and Chris slid off the fertilizer and went inside.

"You get all those cans stamped?" came Mr. Hollander's voice.

"Yes. I made a display with the leftovers down in front. That okay?"

"Sure. Fine. Looks real good." Mr. Hollander came to the screen and peered out. "Thought I heard voices out here. How you, Evie? How's Donna Jean?"

"Still waiting," Evie told him.

"Well, one of these days she'll be busier than a one-armed paperhanger. Tell her to enjoy it while she can."

When Evie went back inside to get her groceries, she saw that Chris had whisked the empty cans and containers out of sight. Even the dangling pie pan had disappeared. She smiled at him when Mr. Hollander wasn't looking, and he smiled back.

"See you around," Chris called when she left.

"Sure."

Halfway down the highway, the "sure" embarrassed her. Couldn't she have thought of something more clever? And her ugly striped tee shirt! Why hadn't she put on the new one?

When she reached the cemetery, she decided to cut through it and enjoy the coolness of the trees. The entrance was back on a side road, so she had to make her way down a steep slope instead, running the last fifteen feet. She came to a stop beside a white granite angel holding an open book, its eyes cast down.

"*Virginia Ruth Mays, 1926–1978*," the inscription read, "*taken in the prime of her life.*"

Evie subtracted the dates in her head as she followed the winding path among the tombstones. Fifty-two years old, the same as Aunt Ida. She wondered if Aunt Ida had ever had a prime at all. Mother's older sister had come to help out when Evie was born and had just stayed on ever since. She had come as a "mail-order Christian," Father called her—a certified member of the Rainbow Revival Church, which ministered by mail. She had a prayer handkerchief, which she laid on her knee when the arthritis was bad, and claimed to have once spoken in tongues. Maybe that was her prime.

There was a heady fragrance of honeysuckle all about her as Evie crossed a narrow stream at the far end of the cemetery—its bank littered with discarded plastic flowers and wreaths—and climbed the hill; the rest of the walk home seemed cooler, shaded by overhanging trees.

"Donna Jean?" she called, setting her sack in the kitchen.

"Evie?"

She went back toward the living room. Donna Jean was down on her hands and knees, biting her lip.

"Donna Jean!"

"It's okay. It was a labor pain. I got down here thinking it would help, and I swear, I don't think I can get back up again."

"Donna Jean!" Evie said again, and felt her own legs grow weak. *No.* She absolutely would not allow herself to act stupid. Forcing her own strength, she knelt down and carefully maneuvered her cousin up on one foot, then the other.

"They started this morning, only so mild and so far apart I didn't even tell Tom. I knew he'd take the day off, and we can't afford it. But now . . . ooh!" She doubled over, Evie grasping her tightly till it passed.

"I'd better get upstairs. It was a strong one that time."

"Shall I call the doctor?"

"Yes, after you get me in bed. Don't bother calling Tom. He'll be home soon, and if you tell him, he'll only drive like a maniac."

They went up one flight, stopping on the landing so that Donna Jean could catch her breath.

"Just think," she said, smiling wanly. "The next time I come down these stairs, I'll be a mother."

When Tom arrived home, the doctor's car was in the clearing. Tom burst through the door and bounded up the stairs two at a time.

Evie busied herself in the kitchen, preparing a cold chicken salad. She could hear no loud moans, and that, at least, was reassuring. But the knocking began in her chest again when Dr. Boyd appeared in the doorway and said, "Well, Evie, it's going to be a while yet. She's fairly comfortable, so I'm going to leave her in your hands and go see another patient while I can."

"*Leave* her?"

"Don't worry. Tom's timing the contractions and knows where to reach me. Go on up and talk with her. She could use the company."

Tom was sitting on the edge of the bed, massaging Donna Jean's back. Her gown had been pulled up so that her belly stuck out, a huge white egg with hardly any navel at all.

"Hi, Evie." Donna Jean modestly pulled the gown down a little. "Come on in."

Evie sat in the rocker self consciously. It seemed like such a private time. The wicker laundry basket, which would serve as the baby's bed for a while, stood ready by the window, Evie's green and yellow quilt folded at one end.

"Now I know what it's like to be in labor," Donna Jean told her. "Boring."

Tom laughed. "She wants entertainment, does she? Evie, can you do the Mexican hat dance? No? Well, we could juggle Pepsi bottles, or I could play my harmonica."

Evie smiled and Donna Jean reached back and patted Tom's hand.

"What would I do without you?" she asked him.

"Well, for one thing, you wouldn't be having this baby," he said, and they all laughed.

There was a strange, heady delight in being here and sharing this experience with them, Evie thought. In this house she was treated as an adult, was in on their jokes. It was as though the three of them together were having the baby.

Mercifully, because of the mulberry tree at the front of the house, the bedroom was cool. The breeze that came in one window and drifted toward the other brought with it the smell of roses.

"Oooooh!" Donna Jean arched her back suddenly, then drew in her breath and held it. When she released it, it came in short jerky spurts, as though she were on the verge of sobbing.

"Easy, now," Tom said.

Evie got up and stood off to one side, her mouth feeling dry and strange, her legs begging for a command, a task. The muscles in her throat tightened.

"Concentrate on your breathing," Tom was saying. "Raise your diaphragm to relieve the pressure. Good. Now pant. Open your mouth and pant."

Donna Jean rolled over on her back, her hair matted to her forehead.

"Good," Tom said. "That's good."

For the next hour, Evie busied herself making cracked ice for Donna Jean to suck and soaked wash cloths in icy water, wringing them and placing them on her cousin's forehead. She felt better when she had something to do and went back and forth from bedroom to kitchen, quiet and efficient.

By seven, the doctor had returned; Tom met him at the top of the stairs.

"The contractions are strong, but they're still six minutes apart and not getting any closer," he said.

"Well, let's have a look."

Evie set the table for dinner, even though she felt sure that no one would be eating. It helped somehow to go through a familiar routine—first the plates, then the silverware, then the glasses. . . . She even put some milk out for the yellow stray cat.

There was a loud cry from upstairs.

"No! Oh, please don't, Dr. Boyd!"

For the first time, Evie's legs buckled beneath her and she slid down against the refrigerator. Her head flopped over on her shoulder. She did not faint, however. She simply felt as though she were deprived of all blood, all strength, and when she realized that she was still conscious, she made her way over to a chair and drew herself up on it.

Tom came down, not looking so good himself.

"What happened?" Evie asked quickly.

"He had to examine her, and it was painful. He thinks the baby's head is turned and that's why we're not getting anywhere." Tom sat down across from Evie and his shoulders slumped. "Whew! I thought I could take anything, but hearing Donna Jean yell like that, I had to get out for a minute."

That made two of them, then. It helped.

The doctor came in. "There's nothing to worry about. I'm going to give that baby a chance to turn its head. Listen, Tom, I was up all night, and I'm dog-tired. I'm going to stretch out on your couch, but it's very important that you wake me in an hour. If the head hasn't turned by then, I'll use forceps."

Tom nodded and turned to Evie. "I'll stay with Donna Jean. You keep an eye on the clock and answer the phone if it rings."

Evie sat across from the clock on the kitchen windowsill. What if she fainted? What if Tom fell into an exhausted sleep and no one woke the doctor till it was too late?

Seven twenty-five. Upstairs, the contractions seemed to be coming more frequently. Each time, Donna Jean's moanings began low and reached a peak, then tapered off again for a few minutes. Evie began timing them herself: five minutes, four minutes, five minutes, seven minutes, four minutes, three minutes. . . .

At eight-fifteen, Tom woke the doctor: "I think something's starting to happen."

Evie sat at the top of the stairs where she could see into their bedroom, her hands cold. She wished that Sue Shields were there—someone as scared as she was. They would hold onto each other when-

77

ever Donna Jean moaned and wonder again if they were ever going to have babies. In consoling each other, they might not feel so helpless.

"Push, honey," she heard Tom say. "You've got to help us along, now."

There were grunting sounds—embarrassing, straining sounds—and Donna Jean's face was all screwed up in her concentration. Evie closed her eyes. She could never make noises like that in front of people, everybody standing around watching her push. Oh lordy, if Sue heard that!

There was another burst of crying, and then Donna Jean sobbed, "Oh, it hurts! It hurts! I don't want this baby."

Evie buried her face in her lap. She would never have a baby, never! Evelyn Hutchins wasn't going to allow herself to go through all this pain and humiliation. She felt hollow with panic, helpless for Donna Jean, and she saw only a childless future for herself. No children, ever, ever!

Dr. Boyd sounded unflustered, however. "That's okay, Donna Jean," he said. "You're doing just fine now, just fine. In a minute, the worst will be over."

Evie pressed her hands over her ears, protecting herself from what was going on in the bedroom. To have gone through all this and not want the baby? To have painted its room, bought its clothes, carried it about for nine months, and then not to care? What a cruel thing a birth was. . . . She found that she was crying.

The tears helped calm her, and finally she lifted her head and leaned back against the wall. At first she heard no sound at all, then panting and huffing and a running murmur of encouragement from the doctor.

Then there was Donna Jean's voice again, clear and excited. "Is it coming? Is it coming?"

"It's coming."

A rollicking nervous laugh. "Really?"

"You're doing great, honey," said Tom.

"A few more good pushes," said the doctor.

Evie got up and stole to the doorway.

"Evie," Tom called softly when he saw her. "Come and watch."

She shook her head and started to back away.

"It's all right, Evie," Donna Jean said weakly. "I want you here."

Despite the trembling of her knees, Evie moved into the room. There, between Donna Jean's legs, through the bulging perineum, was a baby's damp red hair. And then, with another push, Donna Jean forced the head out, up to the eyebrows first, then out to the chin.

"What is it?" she asked excitedly. "I can't see! What is it?"

"Can't tell yet, honey, but it's a redhead!" Tom told her. "Donna Jean, we've got us another redhead!"

Donna Jean began to laugh giddily, and the doctor smiled.

"Don't push now, Donna Jean—just let it slide. Yep, here it comes."

And the baby came flopping, gushing out, covered with a white, curdled goo, its small legs and arms as wrinkled as a blanched prune. The doctor placed it on Donna Jean's chest.

"A boy!" It was not a shout, but a whisper. "A little red-haired boy," Tom said, hugging his wife.

"It's over!" Donna Jean cried happily, as she touched her baby. "I've got a son! Oh, God, I'm so happy! I'm so happy!"

There was a new sound in the room now, a small squeal, like that of a tiny kitten. And Evie remembered the gift she had brought. Shakily, she slipped down the hall for the rubber toy to set in one corner of the newborn's bed.

Six

JOSHUA JOHN RAWLEY.

The miniature fingers, either knotted into fists or stretched stiffly outward. The little pink feet, toes curled under. The head seemed all out of proportion to the rest of the body, as large as the chest, and the lungs, by the end of the first week, no longer confined themselves to pitiful mews, but gave forth lusty, explosive cries of displeasure.

Evie had never realized that something so small, so new to the world, could command such power. One sharp, indignant cry—a bleat, even—would bring the three of them running.

The first few days were only a blur in her memory, with sleep whenever she could find it. Though her room was at the other end of the hall, doors were left open at night to let the breeze through, and each time the baby woke for a feeding, Evie would wake with him and lie listening.

There would be a low, comforting murmur from either Donna Jean or Tom, then the squeak of their bedsprings, followed by the soft pad of feet across the floor to his basket. The cries would reach a crescendo, until suddenly the sound would be muffled, and then all would be still. In the silence that followed, Evie sometimes heard a small belch or a wheeze.

During that first week, she could not bring herself to pick Joshua up. Terrified that one mistake would break a bone, she stayed quite contentedly in the background, embroidering his name on his quilt, and left him to his parents. But he was hers, she felt, almost as much as theirs. It was Evie, next after Tom, who first learned that Donna Jean was expecting; Evie who sat outside the room during labor; and Evie—along with the doctor and Tom—who had witnessed the birth. It was Evie, too, who would watch him grow these first few months, who would notice the smallest changes, the slightest shift of molecules that would turn him from newborn to baby.

And when the normal routine closed in once more and Tom went back to work, it was Evie who walked the floor with Joshua during the afternoons as Donna Jean slept; Evie who laid the small head against her shoulder, soothing a colicky spell; Evie who nuzzled his tiny rosebud ear and drank in his sweet baby scent. When feeding time approached and she could delay him no longer, she would take him to Donna Jean, who would stretch out her arms and say sleepily, "The cafeteria's open, kid; come and get it."

When Tom came home each day, it was conference time, as they called it. He would sit on the sofa with Donna Jean on one side and Evie on the other, resting Joshua against one propped-up knee.

"Well, Senator," he would say, "what's the matter? You seem a bit foggy. Too many receptions, eh? Whoops! A handkerchief, please, a handkerchief! The senator's leaking his lunch."

They would all laugh then as Donna Jean produced the ever-ready towel.

"Now as we were saying, Senator, what do you think about unemployment? Do you think that some people should be allowed to lie around all day just drinking in the milk of human kindness, or do you think that every able-bodied American should. . . ."

A small, prolonged belch from the baby made them weak with laughter.

"I agree completely, Senator," Tom would say as Joshua waved his fists, and then, slipping one hand under his son's back and head, Tom would hug the baby close and say, "Oh, Donna Jean, haven't we got us something wonderful? You going to grow up to make us proud, Josh? Are you, huh?" And then, as the baby turned its head away, "Hey, kid, this is your old man talking. Don't I get a little respect around here?"

People came and went, poking their heads in the door to see if mother and baby were awake, leaving a gift on the hall table if they weren't. There were cellophane-wrapped packages of baby underwear, fancy handmade bibs, and picture albums ready to receive the first photos.

Mrs. Hutchins and Aunt Ida dropped by one afternoon. If Evie's mother had felt slighted because she had not been called upon as midwife, she gave no sign of it. They had come to deliver a small pair of corduroy overalls.

"Aunt Ida, you made these yourself!" Donna Jean exclaimed when she saw them. "These are just the sweetest . . . !"

"Didn't hardly take any time at all." Aunt Ida beamed, then frowned at the way Donna Jean was walking about. "In my day, a woman was kept in bed for two weeks, and she never had no back trouble. Now doctors let 'em up the next morning, and women just aren't as stout as they used to be, not that it's any of my business. What are you taking for tonic?"

"Tonic?"

"For blood! Land sakes, don't tell me the doctor didn't give you nothing for anemia! Well, you don't need no fancy medicine. You tell Tom to bring you a bunch of new nails out of the store, put 'em in a bucket, and pour water over 'em. When that water gets to be rusty, that's your tonic; that'll put the iron back in you. That's what my grandmother used to do."

Donna Jean laughed. "Aunt Ida, you're still at it. Remember, just before my wedding, when you tried to take off my freckles with buttermilk and lemon juice?"

"It would have worked, too, if you'd kept at it." Aunt Ida smiled.

"Sometime this summer," said Mother, "when things have settled down a bit, we'd like you to come over for Sunday dinner."

Donna Jean hesitated. "Maybe around August," she said. "We'll see."

"How's Matt doing?" Evie asked, curiously.

"Surprisingly well, isn't he, Ida? At first Murphy hardly spoke to him, and we thought we'd have a rebellion on our hands. But Matt seems patient, and Murphy's warming up to him."

"Don't count your chickens," warned Aunt Ida.

Outside, Evie's aunt grabbed a hoe and said she was going to give the Rawleys' small garden a few licks before she left, seeing as how it was going untended, and Evie and her mother waited beside the car.

Mrs. Hutchins had a way of looking serene. The more hectic things got around her, the calmer she became. It was as though she had picked this for her life's challenge—to keep her head while everyone about her was losing his. When it came to religious faith, however, she was as intense and fanatical as the disciples themselves.

"I'm certainly hoping we'll be seeing you in church soon, Evie," she said. "Now, of course, I understand that these first few weeks are going to be difficult, but pretty soon you'll work out a schedule."

"Well, it's sort of awkward," Evie told her. "Tom and Donna Jean don't show any inclination to go. Always seems like there's so much to do on Sundays, with all Tom's papers to grade."

Mother sighed. "Before she was married, Donna Jean was as faithful as the rest—every Sunday, there in the same pew."

"I think it's that business about Rose, Mother, and it would have been a kindness if somebody had explained it to me before—if I hadn't had to find it out myself from Donna Jean. She's just not comfortable around Rose, that's why she doesn't come."

Mother dismissed this with a wave of the hand: "There are lots of other pews to choose from." She leaned against the car, arms folded over her ample bosom, her feet, in brown Oxfords, neatly together. "It happens sometimes when folks go off to college. They lose their faith. I don't know what it is exactly that makes them think that what men have to say in their books is more important than what God has to say in His. When I went off for my twelve-month nursing course, I made up my mind I wouldn't listen to a thing that kept me from loving the Lord with all my heart and soul and mind and strength."

"Maybe Tom and Donna Jean do too, but in their own way."

"Well, it's not much of a testimonial if they can't put aside one day a week to glorify Him."

"Mother, I'm not going to tell them that!"

"There are other ways of saying the same thing."

Aunt Ida came back around the house, and Evie wanted to let the conversation drop. The last thing in the world she wanted was to have Aunt Ida leap into the discussion.

But then Mother said, "All you have to do is lead the way, Evie. It wouldn't put your father out any to drive over on Sundays to pick you up and drop you off again after church."

Evie forgot Aunt Ida as a new tension tightened her throat: "Mother, I told you that if I went to Donna Jean's this summer, I wanted you to treat me as though I was a hundred miles off. I want to get the feel of really being on my own. If you're going to come after me every week, I might as well be living with you."

"Well!" Aunt Ida said. "Only three weeks gone, and already she's talking like this!"

But Mother's face softened and she looked at Evie

as though, if words couldn't touch her, she might reach her with her eyes.

"Just stay true to yourself, dear. Don't let anyone turn you into something you're not."

Sue Shields and her mother also came by. After admiring the baby, Sue followed Evie out to the garden and sat on a stump while Evie resumed her bean-picking.

"You're not going to be stuck here all summer, are you?" she asked. "Can't you get away once in a while?"

Evie wiped an arm across her forehead, straddling a row. "Sure, if I want to. Where's there to go?"

Sue smiled through her blue-tinted glasses. "How about Hollander's?"

"Hollander's?"

"Evie, have you *seen* him? Chris Lundgren?"

"I saw him once."

"I've been by there almost every day. I can't keep my eyes off him. And he'll be here all summer!"

"He seemed real nice."

"What did he say?" Sue prodded.

Evie dumped a handful of beans in the basket and went on picking, shooing the ladybugs off the leaves. "Well, I don't remember exactly. Asked if he could help me, I guess."

"Is that all?"

A warning light flickered somewhere in Evie's head. "He told me he played the drums. In fact, he was beating on some old cans when I walked in."

Sue laughed then. "He does that over the lunch hour when Mr. Hollander goes home. Sometimes I sit, and he plays for me. He has a combo back in Silver Spring, you know."

"He must be pretty good."

"He is. He's got a five-piece drum set. A Ludwig. They're the best drums you can buy." Sue slid off the stump and picked a few clusters that Evie had overlooked. "Listen. Let's walk over to Hollander's sometime, real casual—both of us."

"Oh, sure. I'll walk all the way there, dripping with sweat, and say I was just passing by."

"Come on, Evie. We could go over the noon hour and talk to him. It looks too obvious if I keep going by myself. Next week, huh?"

"Maybe," Evie told her.

She sat on the porch steps, Joshua in her lap, observing how—if she leaned a few inches to the left—the sun fell on his face and he squinted. If, holding his scrawny ankles in her hands, she idly ran a finger over the bottom of his bare feet, he jerked slightly and curled his toe under. Whenever anything brushed his cheek, Joshua tried to reach it with his mouth. And touching the mouth itself made it open instantly, like the mouth of a young bird, and then he would sink back into sleep once more, busy with the task of growing.

What a wonder he was, so perfectly formed, this tiny person. The wrinkles were just beginning to fade from his funny bowed legs, and the chest grew larger by the day. What exquisite softness of skin, what fluff of hair, what startling blue eyes lay beneath his puffy lids, how infinitely small the nostrils. . . . Evie felt as though she could spend hours and hours just looking, reveling in this child that, in some unspoken way, seemed hers.

Leaning back against the post with her eyes closed, enjoying the cool-hot mixture of shade and sun on her skin, the heavy warmth of Joshua in her lap, she heard the familiar sound of Murphy's bike coming up the lane from the highway.

She opened her eyes to watch Matt come into view, pedaling slowly, but this time—walking along beside him—was Chris Lundgren.

Evie drew back her legs sharply, her first thought being to dash inside and comb her hair. Joshua startled, waving his fists, his face bunching up into a cry. She chided herself for her carelessness, soothed him into sleep once more, and resigned herself to letting Chris see her as she was.

"Hi," Matt called, unsure of a welcome.

"Hi." It was Chris to whom Evie spoke, however. He smiled shyly at her, loping along, his tall shoulders stooping as though he weren't accustomed yet to his height.

"Smells like a bakery," Matt said, as his nose picked up the buttery cinnamon smell of a cake Donna Jean was making. He leaned his bike against a tree and came over. "You've met Chris, haven't you?"

"Yes."

"This the baby, huh?" Matt leaned down to look. Chris merely peered over his shoulder, looking more at Evie than at Joshua.

"Boy, they sure do come small," Chris said at last.

Evie smiled. "He is tiny, isn't he? But you should hear him yell."

The boys stood awkwardly about a few minutes.

"This all you have to do, just sit around holding the kid?" Matt asked finally.

Evie gave him a disgusted look. "A lot you know about babies. Is this all *you* have to do—ride around on that old bike and make stupid comments?"

Both Matt and Chris laughed.

Chris removed the drumsticks from his back pocket as he sat down on the steps and beat a soft tattoo on the porch floor. "This house is just about out in the middle of nowhere, isn't it?"

"That's what the Rawleys love about it—like a private estate—the cemetery, the woods. . . ." Evie studied him. "You off work?"

"Yeah, I work every day till four, and Saturday mornings. Matt rode by, and we were looking for something to do."

She would never be rid of Matt, ever! Evie thought. Leave it to him to make friends with Chris Lundgren.

Donna Jean came out on the porch. "I thought I heard company." She was still wearing her maternity blouse and skirt, but the swelling in her ankles was gone. "Hi, Matt. Good to see you."

Chris was introduced, and then Donna Jean said, "Listen, I've just baked a cake. As soon as Tom drives up, whistle and I'll bring it out. We'll eat it right here."

At that very moment there came the sound of a car on the lane, and Donna Jean dashed back inside.

"It's him," Evie called.

Just as Tom got out of the car, Donna Jean appeared in the doorway again, carrying a big golden pound cake, its edges beautifully fluted, with a large candle in the center.

"Joshua's two weeks old, everybody," she announced.

They cheered.

Joshua, of course, woke up, and began nuzzling Evie in search of milk. Donna Jean took him to the bench near the door and nursed him while Evie cut the cake.

"Hey! This is a real homecoming!" Tom said.

92

It was pleasant on the porch, one of those moments when everybody seemed relaxed, when conversation came naturally. It would be perfect, Evie was thinking, if Chris had come alone.

"You've got a nice place here," he said.

"Going to be around for a while?" Tom asked.

"Well, usually my dad's transferred every two years. But he says this time it might be four. That's why he rented a house."

Evie's eyes met his. Every summer for the next four years. . . . He would go from seventeen to twenty-one. She tried to imagine what he would look like at twenty-one—more broad-shouldered, sinewed, mustached, his heavy shock of white-blond hair brushed back. . . .

He smiled at her, at the way she was watching him, and her heart thumped in anticipation of the summers to come. And then she remembered Sue Shields.

"You fellas come by more often now," Donna Jean was saying. "I like having Evie's friends about. I can't always promise you a cake, but we've got a cherry tree that's just about ready for picking."

Joshua was squirming uncomfortably, and she transferred him to her shoulder. He burped then and followed it with a coo. Amid the general laughter, Tom said:

"And many happy returns of the day, kiddo."

* * *

Things did not always run smoothly, however. There were days when the small coos of the baby were replaced by an almost incessant crying, when peeved impatience filtered in among their concern.

Once, when Evie was changing Joshua upstairs and Donna Jean was rinsing his diaper—Tom stretched out exhausted on the couch below—the phone rang . . . and rang . . . until Donna Jean yelled in exasperation:

"Tom!"

"All *right!*" he bellowed, and plodded sleepily through the hallway to the kitchen.

Another time, after a humid day made worse by lack of sleep, Tom brought a stack of papers to the table to grade during dinner. They all three sat together, silently picking at their food, and then Joshua began crying again from upstairs.

"Shall I go get him?" Evie asked, knowing by the tone of the howling that it would only become more frantic.

"No, he's got to learn we can't jump every time he takes the notion," Tom said.

And after another length of silence downstairs, squawling from above, Donna Jean complained, "I'd think you could at least save the papers till later, so we could have a normal conversation."

Tom picked them up, dropped them on the floor with a thud, tossed his pen down after them and snapped, "Okay. Let's talk. What do you want to talk about?" Evie found some excuse to leave the kitchen.

And yet, despite their chronic exhaustion, the pressure of summer school teaching, the endless interruptions, and Joshua's nightly colic, love seemed to creep in again by the end of each evening. More often than not, Evie would pass by the living room to see the Rawleys sitting side by side on the couch, their feet sharing the hassock, their arms languid, relaxed.

"The colic won't last forever," Donna Jean said to Evie one afternoon as she sat in the dining room folding the wash. "I've been reading Dr. Spock. He says it's usually gone by the end of the third month, so all we have to do is hang on. What we need, I guess, is a sense of humor. That and a good night's sleep. You ought to get away for a while, Evie—do something with your friends. We all need a break."

"I will. Sue's mother is going to drop her off this afternoon. Maybe we'll go somewhere."

When Sue arrived at two, she looked somehow different. Evie studied her a moment, then opened the screen. "You look like you've got pinkeye."

"Pinkeye!" Sue flounced inside to the mirror at the end of the hall. "It's a five-dollar violet eyeliner stick, that's what."

"Five dollars to look like you've got pinkeye?" Evie stared. She balanced on one bare foot and scratched her knee with the other. "So what do you want to do?"

"Go to Hollander's, like I said."

"Well . . . wait till I get my sneakers." Evie went upstairs, and when she came down, Sue was in the dining room talking with Donna Jean.

"I always wondered what it *really* feels like to have a baby," Sue was saying.

"Lordy, Sue!" Evie said.

But Donna Jean only laughed. "I always wondered that too, and once, when I asked Mother, she said she'd forgotten. Now wasn't that helpful? I figured that it must either have been so awful she didn't want to tell me or so terrible that it gave her amnesia, one or the other."

Evie waited in the doorway.

"Is it like being ripped open?" Sue prodded.

"Good heavens no. It's not a new pain. You've felt it before, just not as strong."

"Like cramps?" Sue absolutely would not shut up.

"Partly. Partly backache and partly like the granddaddy of all belly aches. Yes, I think that was what it was like most of all—a monstrous stomachache that almost made me want to throw up."

"Ugh," said Evie, reaching down to tie her laces.

"It sort of comes in waves, with spaces in between at first, then one right after another near the end. I remember, when each pain began—a rolling, stretching pain—I'd start counting by fives, and by the time I got to eighty, it was the worst. Then it would ease back down. And I remember thinking that it wouldn't be so bad if I could just catch my breath in between."

"Whew!" Sue looked at Evie. "What do you think? Are you going to try it?"

"Not right this minute," Evie told her. "Come on before you ask something *really* dumb."

They set off down the dirt lane, sticking to the side where the sycamores and pine cast their heaviest shade, the road dusty beneath their feet.

"You put on a new tee shirt," Sue said, glancing over.

Evie shrugged. "You were with me when I bought it. Got to wear it some time."

Sue swooped down on a fat purple clover and chewed the stem as she walked. "I met that guy who's staying at your place. He came by the store the other day, and Chris introduced us."

"Yeah?"

"I think he's cute."

"Maybe for you."

"I didn't say for me. I think he's interested in you."

"Well, that's marvelous, but I'm not the least bit interested, anxious, or preoccupied about him at all."

"He seems *nice*," Sue said. "When he talks about

you, his eyes sort of light up, the way Chris's do when he looks at me."

It was enough to make a body sick, Evie thought.

"Matt said he was over to see you last week," Sue said slyly.

That did it. "Sue Shields, Matt just rode over because he and Chris were looking for something to do. Nobody came to *see* me."

Sue stopped in her tracks. "Chris came over?"

"Oh, stop it! Just let life happen, will you? You got me engaged, married, pregnant, and delivered, and the only thing I'm thinking about right now is a soft drink and a place to sit."

They left the dirt lane and started down the shoulder of the highway, setting their sights on the Texaco sign in the distance.

Seven

MATT WAS THERE. Darn! Evie could make him out from far down the highway, he and Chris in the parking lot together, playing Frisbee. As she got closer she could see old Hollander himself sitting in his rusty metal chair, the *Hagerstown Almanack* on his lap, as usual.

Chris was the first to see the girls and stopped— seemingly in midair—letting the Frisbee go sailing by over his head. Evie smiled.

"How do, girls!" Mr. Hollander said, cooling himself with a bamboo fan left over from somebody's funeral. "Sure can hardly wait for that four o'clock breeze to blow in here. Ain't this some July, with all this heat? That's what the wife keeps sayin'." He turned to Evie. "How's Tom's garden doing?"

"Well, it's hard to keep up."

"Should have planted when I told him. He put in

the seed on a new moon, and them beans'll all go to vine."

"I don't know how you can stand to play Frisbee!" Sue said to Chris. "Don't you just feel you're going to wilt?" Her voice had a singsong quality that Evie thought ridiculous.

"Oh, it's not so bad." Chris smiled. "Cleans out the sweat glands."

"Back in the old days," began Mr. Hollander, "my brother and I used to play catch in the cow pasture. We'd get so sweaty that the cows would just mosey over and lick the salt off our arms."

"Oh, gross!" squealed Sue. Evie and Chris exchanged glances.

"Yep. My mother used to say we didn't need us a salt lick for the cows—all we needed was Herbert and me to play catch in the pasture." He went on fanning himself, then called out, "Horse troughs! Anybody know about horse troughs?"

"Have anything to do with horse feathers?" Chris joked, and Sue shrieked again. Evie studied her curiously.

Mr. Hollander laughed. "Come on, Matt, you're a farmboy now. Show this here city kid some learnin'. What's a horse trough?"

"Something I go climb in behind the barn when nobody's looking," said Matt, and they all laughed.

"Oh my, yes, we used to do that," Mr. Hollander told them. "On a hot day we just couldn't stand no more, us kids would take off our shoes and climb in—overalls, dresses—didn't matter. Water come up to the armpits of the tallest boy but the chins of the youngest, and we'd have to keep watch they didn't go under. Why we thought we was rich, don't you know, with our own private swimming pool. Never knew nothing finer, so we thought we had it all."

The phone jangled from inside, and Mr. Hollander rose from his chair and went to answer. He came out a minute later, red in the face and mad as a dog with a bent leg.

"That blamed fool driver left a quarter beef at the meat locker 'stead of bringin' it here. Now I got to go get it myself. Chris, you look after things." He climbed in the old battered station wagon and tore off, tires squealing. Evie would have preferred that he stay. She felt uncomfortable around Chris with Sue there.

"Party! Party!" Matt joked when the wagon had disappeared.

Chris reached in his pocket and took out some quarters, feeding them into the soft drink machine. He handed Evie an orange soda and Sue a Pepsi.

"Oh, thank you!" Sue warbled.

"Big spender," said Matt.

Chris came over and sat down near Evie on the top step and her pulse quickened. "How's the baby doing?"

"Well, Joshua's been crying a lot. Colic, I guess."

"How would you like to go through life with a handle like that?" Matt asked Chris. "Joshua. As in Jericho."

"They've already started calling him Josh," said Evie. "That's not such a bad name. Joshua John."

"Joshua John!" Matt rolled his eyes.

"So what's *your* middle name?" Evie said curtly. "Matthew what?"

His face colored.

"Hey!" Chris said, punching Matt playfully. "What is it? Gladstone? Mortimer? Matthew Mortimer Jewel?"

"Twenty questions!" Sue called out, as Matt's color deepened. Evie watched what she had started and was glad of it. High time Matt had a taste of his own medicine. "Is it the name of a president?"

"No." Matt yanked off his tee shirt and mopped his face with it, tilting his head back to let the breeze fan his neck.

"Somebody in sports?" asked Chris.

Matt shook his head.

Knowing Matt's mother, Evie guessed that his middle name, like his first, had been taken from the Bible. "Is it from the New Testament?"

Matt shrugged. "I don't know."

"The old?"

His color deepened.

"Daniel?"

"Lamentations? Ezekiel?" Sue giggled.

"Jeremiah," guessed Evie.

Matt took a deep breath. "You got it."

Chris whistled. "Whew! Matthew Jeremiah Jewel! Now that's something!"

Evie laughed loudly with the others, enjoying Matt's discomfort.

"I was named after my father, actually," Matt explained. "They called him Jerry." He got up suddenly and hopped down into the parking lot, picking up stones and zinging them across the highway at the signboard on the other side.

"Oh, it's lovely here," Sue said with a sigh from on top the bags of fertilizer. She swung one bare leg back and forth, her toenails painted a bright pink.

"Empress of the Fertilizer." Chris smiled.

"Queen of the Dung," said Matt. No one could accuse Matthew Jeremiah Jewel of flattery.

"What we ought to do is have a picnic," said Chris. "I could probably borrow Dad's car some weekend."

"That's a super idea!" said Sue. "Isn't that a marvelous idea, Evie? Chris and I could bring the hamburger and charcoal, and you and Matt could bring the drinks and dessert."

Evie rested her chin in her hands, furious at Sue. She stared out across the road, beyond the field where there had once been a traveling carnival.

That and an occasional revival meeting were about the only excitement there was in Branbury. Was this the way you got engaged? she wondered. One of your friends just hooked you up with somebody at a picnic, and even if you couldn't stand him, you were his girl before you knew it. Then your picture was in the newspaper in LaPlata, and people started sending you crystal butter dishes?

"Who will bring the blanket?" Sue was saying. "Do you think we'll need a cooler? Who's got a cooler?"

Evie was aware of Chris looking at her, and she glanced over. His eyes seemed so searching that she was convinced he had known what she was thinking.

Mr. Hollander's station wagon came grinding up the road again, a raw hindquarter of steer sticking out the rear window. He was still angry.

"Chris, you got to help me haul this thing to the back room. We got to get it cut up and into the freezer."

Both Chris and Matt went over to help.

"It's so gross!" Sue squealed again. "Could I watch, Mr. Hollander, if I promise not to faint or anything?"

"Listen," Evie said to her, "I'm going back to Donna Jean's."

"Okay," Sue said obliviously. "I told Mother I'd be waiting here anyway." She ran up the steps to hold the screen open as Mr. Hollander and the boys maneuvered the meat inside, and Evie slipped away.

She walked back along the highway, cutting over toward the cemetery on the other side, struggling to get her peevishness under control. What she needed was a simple life without complications. She remembered a quotation she had copied in one of her journals, from a narration of Black Elk: *Is not the sky a father and the earth a mother and are not all living things, with feet and wings or roots, their children?* That was what she wanted to be—a daughter of the earth, living in harmony with the land and sky, involved in no silly triangles with Chris Lundgren and Sue Shields. She would also like to live on the other side of the world from Matt Jewel.

She jumped over the ditch and started down the slope into the cemetery below. As the angle grew sharper, she began to run and came to rest at last beside the statue of the angel holding the open book.

There were more sounds of running footsteps behind her, however, and when she turned, she saw Matt.

"What is it?" Evie asked, annoyed.

He shrugged. "Just decided to split. Figured that old steer had suffered enough without three people hacking away at his hind quarter."

Evie was tempted to smile, but didn't. "Well, I thought Donna Jean might need me."

They wound around through the grave markers, barely disturbing the occasional sheep that blocked the path, and Evie wished with all her heart that Matt would turn around and go back.

"You didn't seem to go much for that picnic idea," Matt ventured.

"It was just the way Sue was organizing it—like a drill sergeant or something."

"Yeah. She reminded me of your aunt. All I have to do is sit down for a minute and she's at me. 'Have you done this?' 'Did you finish that?' "

"Seems to me you *do* have a lot of time on your hands."

"Well, your dad and I have an understanding. I keep a record of the hours I work. As long as I put in forty a week, he doesn't care when it's done. Ida, though, she's even worse than I remembered her."

"You haven't improved any yourself," said Evie.

There was the steady clink of a shovel from down the path. The gravedigger was about. Evie looked for him as they rounded a bend. He was standing waist-deep in a half-dug grave.

"It's Frank Kettle," Evie told Matt.

The man leaned his shovel against one corner of the grave and hoisted himself up to the rim, welcoming the break, tipping back his dirty gray cap.

"You one of the Hutchinses' gals, ain't you?"

"Yes." Evie returned the smile he gave them, which exposed the toothless side of his mouth.

"I thought so. Wilma?"

"No. She's the one who married. I'm Evie."

"Yeah, that's right. They was the three of you. Reckon your pa's preached over most half the folks that's buried here."

"I suppose so. This is Matt Jewel, Frank. He's helping my dad this summer."

Frank grinned a welcome. "You ain't the boy used to live around here seven, eight years ago, are you? Always creatin' a ruckus?"

"That's him," said Evie.

"Whose sheep?" asked Matt.

"Conklin's," the gravedigger told him. "He just turns 'em loose, and no one cares 'cause they save the price of mowin' the grass."

Evie looked down at the gaping hole beyond her feet. It seemed rather indelicate to ask, but she did anyway: "Whose grave?"

Frank Kettle patted the ground beside him. "This here's for a young man up by White Plains. A motorcycle accident, they say. Down near Bel Alton it happened. One moment he was here and plannin' what to do tomorrow, and the next moment there weren't no tomorrow at all. You never know when you take your shoes off if it'll be you or the undertaker what puts them on again." He looked up at Matt. "You ride a motorcycle?"

"No."

"That's good."

The gravedigger leaned forward and grasped the shovel again, resting his arms on the handle. "Funny thing, you know—death always seems to come in threes. Won't be no graves for a while, then one'll come along and soon after, two more. This is the first grave in a long spell, so it makes you wonder, don't it?"

No, not particularly, Evie thought as they walked on. Both Sister Ozzie and Mr. Schmidt could pass away any time, and they weren't the only old folks in Branbury.

"He sounds like your Aunt Ida," Matt told her. " 'Trouble comes in threes,' that's what she always says. If you wait long enough, everything comes in threes. Just depends how you figure it. Same with prayer."

"What's prayer got to do with it?" Evie felt a familiar uneasiness pushing against her chest. She hoped that Matt wasn't planning to walk all the way back with her. Whatever he had to say, she didn't want to hear it. And yet . . . she had asked.

"If you pray for something and get it, God heard your prayer. You don't get? You weren't sincere enough, maybe. Or you prayed for the wrong thing. There's always an excuse." He sauntered along, picking a leaf here and there from a low-lying branch. "I really got your mom ticked off the other morning. She was talking about prayer and faith, and I said, 'Mrs. Hutchins, I could tell you I believed there was a big golden grasshopper up in the sky that whenever I prayed, it heard me—and you couldn't prove it one way or the other.' You know what she did, Evie? You think she'd discuss it with me? She got right down on her knees—right there by the refrigerator—and prayed for Jesus to forgive me. Man! Talk about embarrassing!"

Evie tried not to listen. "We belong to Faith Gospel because we know it's the right religion. We just feel it in our hearts."

"Yeah, and if you were raised in some other church, you'd say *that* was right. Catholic, even."

"I would not!" Evie cried indignantly.

"Yeah? You ever thought about what you believe, or do you just swallow it whole? Why can't I believe in my grasshopper, then?"

"You make me sick," she said, her confusion mounting. "All you do is go around trying to tear things down, Matt Jewel."

"It's not that I *want* to tear things down, Evie. I just can't stand to see people believe in something they don't even try to understand."

She made no reply, walking swiftly ahead as though she couldn't get back to Donna Jean's fast enough.

"You know all that stuff I used to do back in your dad's church? That was part of it. I had questions even then; and if there's one thing you can't have in Faith Gospel, it's questions. My kind, anyway.

Maybe when I get to college and study philosophy, it'll all make sense."

You could *so* have questions, Evie thought desperately. It was the answers that bothered her. Mother usually answered by quoting a Bible verse or even a line from a hymn, and Evie used to pretend that that was enough. But down underneath. . . .

They came to the end of the path where the slope rose sharply again, leading through a tangle of honeysuckle to the lane above. Matt went first and, turning around, extended a hand to Evie, but she had already pulled herself up.

"You going to college?" he asked her.

She didn't know whether to answer or not. "Tom says I should, to get a degree," she said finally. "I'd be the first college graduate in my family. But . . . I don't know. I don't think Mother likes the idea. There's a lot to think about."

"Yeah, that gets to me sometimes—all the decisions. College? Technical school? The Navy? What I'd really like to do is go out west and raise horses or something. But I suppose it wouldn't be anything like I imagine. Things never are."

He stopped abruptly on the lane, hands in his pockets, shoulders hunched. "Well, I'd better get back. I've got to finish some work at your place. See you around, Evie."

He turned and went back down the lane, and Evie walked swiftly on to the Rawleys'. She could not even describe how she felt. All she knew was that whenever she was around Matt Jewel, it was as though he took something from her, and the emptiness inside seemed to grow.

Joshua got his first bath that night. The basin was ready on the kitchen table. The talcum, cotton, and oil were there. The towels were close at hand, and the water had been checked by at least two people, possibly three. Tom straddled a chair, arms resting on the top, camera cocked.

"Oh, Tom, I'm scared!" Donna Jean said as she gingerly lifted the baby up, one hand under his bottom, the other under his head. "What if he slips and rolls over or something? He'll be neurotic for life! He'll get water in his lungs and have pneumonia!"

"He's going to love it. Stick him in."

"Hold the basin, Evie, so it doesn't slide," Donna Jean said, and then, masking her worry, crooned, "Baby's first bath! Josh is going to get his very first bath!"

Evie gripped the basin as Joshua was lowered into it, one pink foot brushing her hand. As soon as he sensed the water on his back, however, he startled, then tensed.

"He doesn't like it!" Donna Jean cried. "Look at him, Tom! He's so rigid."

The baby flailed his arms, his legs as stiff as bed

slats, and water splashed all over the three of them. He yelped and kicked.

Donna Jean jerked him out and held him against her, tears in her eyes.

"He got water on my lens!" Tom kept saying.

Evie took a towel and mopped up the table and floor so they wouldn't all slip and kill themselves. She kept her head turned to hide the fact that she was laughing.

"He hates it!" Donna Jean was weeping. "His first bath, and he hates it!"

"All over my lens, and my pants, too!" Tom said again.

"Listen," Evie said finally, "it's just an idea, but try putting Josh in tummy first, Donna Jean. Keep your hand under his chest so he doesn't wobble so much."

Donna Jean continued to sniffle, wiping one arm across her face.

"One more try," Tom said. "All I've got so far is a picture of both of you howling."

Donna Jean smiled a little. "Okay, Josh, old boy," she said, turning him over. "We're going to go for it."

Evie held the basin again, and Donna Jean lowered the baby, pausing to let him get a feel of the water on his hands and knees before going any further. He cooed once, splashed, looked startled, then cooed again. The camera snapped.

"Hey, I think he's smiling, Donna Jean!" Tom cried. "Look! Look at him, Evie! He's smiling."

"He *does* like it!" Donna Jean let the baby rest his legs against the bottom of the basin while she kept his head and chest up. "Oh, Josh, you darling! He's not afraid of it, Tom."

Joshua gave little grunts of contentment and kicked his legs again.

"He's going to be a swimmer!" said Tom. "Look at him! Look at those thighs! See the power in those legs!"

Evie's sides ached again with contained laughter. How could two intelligent adults carry on so?

"Did I hear a knock?" Donna Jean asked suddenly.

They listened. It came again.

"Oh, Lord, someone's been out there on the porch all this time listening to this nonsense," she cried. "Evie, will you go?"

Evie made her way through the darkened hallway. Someone was silhouetted against the yellow moon, but she could not see the face.

"Hello?" she called, and looked out the screen.

It was Chris.

Eight

"HI," HE SAID.

Against the moonlight, the edges of his hair shone white, like a wreath about his head. Evie opened the screen.

"Hi. You want to come in?"

He rocked back and forth on his heels. "I was wondering if you could come out."

"Uh . . . sure. Just a minute till I tell Donna Jean."

She went back through the hallway, conscious of the way she must look in her wet shirt and cut-offs.

"It's Chris," she said from the doorway. "He wants me to come out for a while."

Tom looked up. "Sure."

"Where you going?" Donna Jean was veiled in a cloud of talcum as she diapered Joshua.

114

"I don't know. Just sit on the porch, maybe."

"Okay."

"You busy doing something?" Chris asked, when she returned.

"We just finished giving Joshua his first bath. You should have seen it. I'm still soaked."

He laughed. Then he stood waiting, arms dangling. Evie took the initiative and sat down on the top step.

"Did the steer ever get cut up?" she asked.

"Oh . . . yeah." He smiled as he sat down beside her. "I discovered something. I don't want to be a butcher."

Laughter.

"I never saw Mr. Hollander so upset," she said.

"Well, he gets that way now and then, but most of the time he's easy." There was a pause. "Wouldn't surprise me if he'd told that driver to take the beef to the locker and then forgot about it."

More laughter. Evie wondered how long it took to get where you didn't laugh all the time—when silences weren't scary. From inside, she could hear happy exclamations from Donna Jean, a quiet murmur from Tom, footsteps, Joshua's soft coo.

"You like it here?" Chris asked.

"I like it fine. A lot different from home. More relaxed, I guess." That sounded rather bold, Evie thought.

"Matt was telling me about your place. Sounds wild."

"Not really. Don't believe a thing *he* tells you."

"What's your dad do?"

"He's a minister."

"No kidding?"

"No kidding."

"He strict with you?"

It was the first time Evie had really considered the question. She shrugged. "Never anything I wanted to do that I couldn't. What's your dad like?"

"Well, he doesn't have a whole lot to say. We both like to bowl. Do that on weekends, sometimes. We get along okay."

Was it polite, Evie wondered, to ask about his mother? When two people were divorced, could you mention them in the same breath?

"What's it like where you live in Silver Spring?" she asked instead.

"Oh, you can't really tell it from Wheaton on one side or Takoma Park on the other. They all run together."

"You and your mom live alone?"

"And a brother. He works for IBM."

A light came on inside, making a square of yellow on the porch, then went off again. Footsteps. Voices. Chris told her about his high school, the Blair basketball team, the school newspaper, Spanish. . . . Evie slapped at a mosquito, but could already feel the itchy swell of its bite on her knee.

"Anybody want some lemonade?" came Donna Jean's voice from behind the screen.

"No, thanks," said Chris. "You want some, Evie?"

"No."

Donna Jean disappeared.

"Listen, you want to walk, so you won't be a sitting target for mosquitos?" Chris asked, noticing.

They walked slowly, making it last. There really wasn't anywhere to go except down the lane to the highway and back, but it was a nice walk, secluded and cool. Their bodies grazed each other's as they sauntered along, separated, then touched again. She could almost feel the hair on her arms rise up when she sensed Chris near her.

They stopped once, halfway to the road, to listen to a mockingbird going through its repertoire. Every so often it would throw in the plaintive cry of a catbird, and then they would laugh. The whole earth seemed drenched in the fragrance of honeysuckle, which made a jungle of itself on fence and bush alike.

At the end of the lane they paused somewhat awkwardly, watching a few cars go by. Then, taking their cue from each other, they did a slow turn and started the journey back. This time, however, when their hands touched accidentally, Evie felt his strange long fingers grope for hers and then take her hand in his own. How easy it had been, how simple and natural.

It did not seem necessary to talk any longer, to

fill up space. It was enough that their arms were touching, and Evie felt Chris's thumb gently caress the edge of her hand as he walked her to the door.

There was hardly a minute she was not thinking about Chris. If, for a moment, she forgot him and then he entered her mind again, her heart jumped as though he had just stepped up behind her and put his hands over her eyes.

It was not any one thing that exhilarated her— not the touch of his hand against hers or the caress of his thumb or the way his arm had encircled her waist there, at last, in the pine-scented darkness. Not even the way his lips had grazed her forehead when he said good night on the porch. It was the easy way that it had all happened, one thing gliding into the next. Everything was easier here. She tried to imagine Chris calling on her back at the Hutchinses' place, with Aunt Ida about, Rose, Sister Ozzie. . . . The scene came to a standstill.

When Chris came again the second night, both he and Evie were smiling. There was no awkward pause at the door, no quips or wisecracks. None of the silly teasing, like Clyde Harrigan did back in seventh grade, bringing her a box of Whitman chocolates and then laughingly jerking them away just out of reach. Evie simply went out on the porch and they walked hand in hand to the spot where the mockingbird had sung the night before, laughing to find him in concert once again.

Donna Jean's request the following day for a container of sour cream and some nutmeg brought an instant offer from Evie to go for them at once, and when she turned onto the highway from the lane, the Texaco sign didn't seem half as far as it used to.

She was smiling to herself, thinking how Chris would look when she surprised him, glad for the extra bonus of seeing him again so soon. She hardly heard the car behind her slowing down until a voice called out.

"Hey, good-looking! Come on, get in!"

Something told her not to panic as she turned, and then she saw him. "Dad!" She laughed.

She slid onto the seat and gave him a quick hug. "I'm only going as far as Hollander's."

"Well, then, I'll drive real slow and make it last."

"Where've you been?"

"Went to see a family down near Pisgah. Mighty lot of trouble in that house, but they've put it in God's hands and I think He'll see them through." He glanced over. "How's the shop coming?"

"We've hardly had time to think about it with Josh around. Donna Jean would like to have it finished by October so folks could buy their Christmas presents from us."

When her father made no reply, Evie asked, "Does it bother you, Dad?"

"What?"

"My going into business with Donna Jean."

The way he didn't answer for a moment answered for him. Yet his words said something else. "No point in letting it bother me, honey. If that's what you want to do, it's not me who should be saying different."

She tried translating it in her head. "What would you rather I did?"

"Oh, now, you oughtn't to ask me that."

The Texaco sign loomed larger and the car slowed down even more.

"No, go on. Pretend I was a toad or something and you could change me into anything. What would I be? A doctor? A concert violinist? What?"

"My own Evie, that's all."

"You're stalling, Dad."

The familiar slow smile spread across his face again, beginning at the base of his nostrils and working across the leathery face in both directions.

"Well, if it was up to me, and *you* were agreeable, I think I'd be partial to having a lady preacher in the house."

She turned and stared at him. "A preacher!"

"I didn't think you'd fancy it."

"A *preacher?*" She had to say it again to make sure. Once, when she was very small, she remembered standing up by the pulpit of the little stucco church and shouting out the names of hymns, just to get the feel of it. She had never been so inclined again.

He reached over and patted her knee. "I can see it doesn't set well on you."

"I never thought about it, to tell the truth."

Mr. Hutchins pulled the car onto the gravel in front of Hollander's and parked to one side.

"Well, like I said, it's only a fancy. Can't blame me for wanting the pulpit to pass to one of my kin. But you've got to do whatever it is you were meant for, Evie."

Somehow that made it too official. She wasn't entirely sure she was "meant" to sell quilts in a shop with Donna Jean for the rest of her natural life. It was just the best thing on the horizon at the moment. She had her senior year ahead of her when she'd be working with Donna Jean after school. Then, when she graduated and became a real partner, she'd see. An old faded billboard behind Hollander's said *Jesus Saves, Heals, and Delivers.*

A preacher? Evie thought again.

Her father seemed in no hurry to let her go. "Sure don't see too much of you lately, honey. Guess this is better than nothing."

"Everybody's mad at me because I haven't brought the Rawleys back to church," Evie said. "It's like I was sent to fight the Philistines or something instead of to take care of Josh."

Her father laughed. "I don't want you fighting anybody, honey. Enough going on in the world as it is."

"Why is everybody so upset about them, then? As far as I can see, Donna Jean and Tom live good, decent lives. Aunt Ida said once, though, that this didn't matter unless you were saved. She said the only thing that will get you to heaven is faith."

"Well," said Mr. Hutchins, "I'd like to see the Rawleys back in church—I don't deny that. But it seems to me we ought not to worry so much about folks who don't believe and still manage to live by Christ's example and worry a little more about folks who say they believe and then go join the devil."

Evie liked that. She leaned over and kissed him, then hopped out and closed the door. But the car didn't move immediately, and she could feel her father's eyes on her as she went up the steps and opened the screen.

Thursday, after dinner, Evie heard hammering and found Tom hanging an old two-seater swing from the porch ceiling.

"Where did this come from?" she asked.

"It's been in the shed out back ever since we moved in. Just never got around to putting it up." A smile played about his lips. "If you're going to be courted, Evie, we have to do it proper."

"Oh, for heaven's sake," she said, and went back inside.

Nonetheless when Chris came over shortly afterwards, they sat in it and enjoyed the rhythm of the swinging, while the yellow stray watched from the window ledge.

Joshua was lying back in a secondhand stroller, wide awake, entertained by an orange paper flower that Donna Jean had wired up on the tray in front of him. Evie had her feet hooked onto the front of the stroller, so that it moved back and forth with the swing. Josh burbled contentedly, his little head wobbling from side to side.

"Look at him," Chris said, as the baby stared transfixed at the flower, a thin trickle of drool running down his chin. Joshua waved his arms up and down and stretched out his legs in a seeming rush of delight. Then his eyes crossed, his head tipped to one side, and he lost his focus on the flower, only to find it once again blooming there before him.

Evie and Chris giggled as they watched, and at the sound of their laughter, the baby's eyes would orbit about once more. Sometimes he seemed to stare with great interest at his fist and, when it moved, would startle as though it were something unattached.

Matt's bicycle appeared in the clearing. He stopped, staring up at the porch.

"Hey, Matt! How you doing?" Chris called, and went on pushing his feet against the floor, one arm around Evie's shoulder.

Slowly Matt let the bike drop on the ground and came over, standing awkwardly on the steps.

"Look." Evie pointed. "We think Josh has discovered his fist."

But Josh had found the paper flower again and smiled his silly grin.

"Your *fist*, dummy!" Chris laughed. "That thing in your hand, remember? What you bopped yourself with a minute ago?"

"Hey, who's making fun of my kid?" Tom came out on the porch and whisked Joshua up, high over his head, tilting him so that they were eyeball to eyeball. "How you doin', kiddo? Want your old man to take you away from all this?"

In answer, a dribble of saliva landed on Tom's face, and this got another laugh.

"Bedtime," Tom said, folding Joshua in his arms. "Thanks for rocking him, Evie."

"So what's new?" Chris asked Matt.

"I've been looking all over for you. Hollander said you were probably here."

"Yeah. I like the scenery." Chris grinned. Matt didn't.

"I was thinking about that picnic," Matt said. "Wondered if you all were still interested. Nothing else much to do."

"If I can get Dad's car," Chris said. "What about Saturday afternoon? Could you go, Evie?"

It was not that Evie had forgotten Sue. The moment she had seen Chris standing outside the screen a few nights before, her joy had been tempered by the hurt she knew Sue would feel. But in the heady days that followed, she had pushed it into a far corner of her mind, reasoning that Sue would gradually get the message from Chris himself and lose interest.

"Sure," she said, faking enthusiasm. "Why not?"

"Great!" Chris looked around. "Who'll tell Sue?"

"Matt will," Evie said quickly.

"Put her in charge of hamburgers and tell her I'll pick her up around three."

They discussed then what the rest of them would bring, and Evie continued pushing against the floor of the porch with leaden feet.

On Friday morning she baked a cake and thought about calling Sue. Something needed to be said before the picnic. *Sue*, she would say, *I just thought you ought to know that Chris and I have been seeing each other*. But she spent the afternoon in the yard with Donna Jean, and the call was never made.

"Do you believe in God?" she asked suddenly, snapping off the young leaves of a dandelion plant and dropping them in the basket. Donna Jean was working on the other side of Joshua, whose infant seat had been turned so that the sun did not shine in his eyes. He slept with his head tipped to one side.

Donna Jean thought for a moment:

"A few years ago, I might have said no. Or I might have said yes, but He doesn't believe in me. Now I say, I think so but I don't understand Him."

When Evie made no comment, she asked, "Why?"

"Just thinking, that's all—about college, actually. Mother said that sometimes when people go to college, they lose their faith."

Donna Jean smiled a little and went back to filling her skirt with dandelions. "Well, of course, I only had two years of it. Tom graduated, so I guess you'd better ask him."

"Be serious."

"The most important thing I learned in college, Evie, is that there are a lot of things in this world for which we don't have answers. Some people can't live with that, but I can."

"You don't believe, then."

"I don't *disbelieve*. I'm perpetually curious, that's all." Donna Jean stood up, clutching her skirt full of dandelions and came over to drop them in the basket, then stared down at the leaves Evie had collected: "You threw away the flowers!"

"Well, of course. Don't you want the greens?"

"I use the blossoms to make our Christmas wine."

"Wine!"

Donna Jean dropped down on the ground. "Oh, lordy, Evie. It never occurred to me how you might feel about that."

Evie sat back on her heels and looked at the yellow flowers strewn about the grass. Only a few days before she had been discussing her faith with her father, and here she was, about to make wine.

"I don't want you to do anything that your parents wouldn't like," Donna Jean told her. "You take care of the greens for supper, and I'll collect the flowers." She went about picking up the yellow blossoms that Evie had discarded. "We ferment them with raisins and oranges and make just enough for the holidays. It's sort of a tradition, Tom's and mine."

The holidays! Wine for Christmas! That was even worse. Evie silently took the basket over to the wash pan on the back stoop and dumped the greens in, swishing them around, rubbing them against each other.

"We must seem awful to you," Donna Jean said finally. "No prayers at mealtime, no church on Sundays, wine at Christmas. . . . I can imagine what Aunt Ida and your mother say about us."

"They don't say much of anything, Donna Jean. They remember you in prayer, that's all."

"Well, it certainly can't make me more confused than I am."

"Aunt Ida would probably say that anything you need to understand, you can find in the Bible."

"Well, I've got news for Aunt Ida: there are a whole lot of questions the Bible doesn't answer."

"Like what?"

"Like why my mother died." Donna Jean came over and sat down. "It was in the fog one night, coming home from prayer meeting. Did you ever know that, Evie? Three of the four women in the car were killed, the fourth had a broken pelvis. The couple in the other car, newlyweds, were killed too."

"Did you blame God for that?" Evie asked.

"No." Donna Jean's voice was low, controlled. "But do you know what that woman said, the one who lived? When she found out that she was the only one of the six alive, she said that God must have saved her for a purpose."

"And that made you angry?"

"It made me *think*, Evie. If God's saving that woman was a miracle, then letting the others die was terrible. And because I can't believe God would do that, it seems most honest to say that I don't understand Him. I'm at peace with myself. Not with Aunt Ida, maybe, or even your parents—but with myself."

"What will you tell Josh when he asks about God?"

"The truth: that I don't know. Do you really think that God would condemn me because I'm being honest, because I don't say things just to save my soul? What a cheap thing *that* is—people going around mouthing 'I believes' just because they're afraid of what might happen if they don't."

Evie spread the greens out on a towel to dry. "What does Tom think? He used to come to our church sometimes, before you both stopped coming."

"He says if there *is* a God up there—powerful,

loving, and supremely intelligent—then He knows exactly how we feel and why. And that all He expects of us is to somehow make the world a better place than it was before we came."

It sounded so right. And yet—on Sunday mornings—the things her father said sounded right as well.

"It was a mutual decision to stop coming, Evie— not just Tom's. Partly it was Rose, and what had happened, and partly just our own doubts about what we believe. But nothing's final, you know. We look at ourselves as explorers. Perhaps our questioning will bring us back to the church later on. Or some other church. We'll have to see."

Joshua yawned and stretched in the afternoon sun, blinking his eyes once or twice, then closing them again.

"Well," Donna Jean said, wiping her hands on her skirt. "It's amazing how easily I can talk to you, Evie." She gathered up the flowers for the infamous Christmas wine. "Bring Josh in, will you?"

Evie cradled the infant seat in her arms. What did Joshua know of God or the universe or even himself? Nothing at all. Perhaps Matt was right. If Josh had been born into a Catholic family, he might learn to say his 'Hail Mary's.' If he had been born a Moslem, he might pray with his face to the east. His mind was like a new journal, just waiting for the pages to be filled. He would believe whatever his parents told him, because parents were supposed to be right. What did God think of so many people arguing with each other over who was right, Evie wondered—killing each other over the centuries in His name?

She gently brushed off a leaf that had lodged on the baby's shoulder. His hair was like fuzz; the closed eyelids a thin film over new-blue eyes.

"I'm just like you, Josh," she whispered. "I don't know any more than you do, and I wish I could be just the way you are now—trusting and happy and not worrying my head about things I don't understand."

If there *was* a God, she thought—and the very fact that an "if" had crept in bothered her—He must have sent Josh to her as symbol. Of what, she wasn't sure. Maybe to let her know that she could start all over and find God in her own way.

She carried the baby slowly to the house. A small bubble formed at the opening between his lips, rising and falling with each breath. Now and then his fingers twitched or a small foot jiggled, and it seemed to Evie that his mouth stretched into a slight smile, then retracted once again.

"I love you so, Joshua," she whispered.

It was something quite different from what she felt for her parents or sisters or for Donna Jean and Tom. Or even Chris Lundgren. Something powerful, and she had never felt it quite as strongly as she did then.

Nine

EVIE WRAPPED THE TOWEL around her head and answered the phone. Sue had already called twice since Matt had phoned her, and each time, her voice sounded like a teakettle. Each time, Evie resolved to tell her about Chris and herself, but the courage never came.

"What are you wearing?" Sue asked this time. "We'll roast in jeans. I've got these new shorts with the braided belt."

"Sue, there are chiggers all over. Wear jeans."

"I know why Matt's so excited about this picnic," Sue said. "He wants to see *you* again."

Tell her, tell her, something bleated inside Evie, but she could not.

"Sue, will you stop that? I don't even like him. I *never* liked him. Just being around him upsets me to death."

"Why? What's so awful?"

"It's what he says. He followed me home from Hollander's the other day and was tearing down my religion."

"Honestly?"

"He gets me all confused. He said if I'd been born into a Catholic home, I'd be Catholic right now."

"Oh, you *wouldn't!* As soon as you got older, you'd know right away it was wrong. You might be a Methodist, but not a Catholic."

Evie sighed. "Sometimes I feel that I'm the only person in the world who can't just say 'I believe' and not worry about it."

"All you have to believe is the Bible, Evie."

"But why not the Koran or the Talmud or something? That's what gets to me."

"What's a talmud?"

"The Jews' book."

"Oh, Evie, you'll go right straight to hell if you talk like that."

Evie stood in front of the mirror drying her hair. Well, so much for telling Sue about Chris. So much for having an intelligent conversation, either. She blew her hair upward till she looked like a woman in the shampoo ads, leaping across a meadow in slow motion. Unlike the women on TV, however, her hair did not stay fluffy when it fell, but drooped listlessly about her shoulders, the way she felt inside. If only she and Chris were having this picnic alone.

At three, the Chevy came up the lane and turned around in the clearing. Matt was in the back seat and Sue, wearing a tee shirt that read, "Surf Naked," was sitting up front beside Chris. She was hanging halfway out the window, merrily tying her scarf to the antenna.

Evie took a deep breath and went out on the porch, carrying the picnic basket. Chris hopped out and came around to put it in the trunk.

"I made a cake." Evie smiled.

'A cake!" Chris shouted. "Hey, we got us a cake! Chocolate?"

"Uh-huh."

He gave her a hug, but Sue didn't see. In Chris's absence she had moved over into the driver's seat and was lightly tapping the horn.

"Come on, get in!" she giggled. "I'm driving this thing."

Chris laughed a little as he went back around.

"Out!" he said, opening the door.

"I can drive!" Sue insisted, in a mock pout. "I've got a learner's permit. You can sit right beside me and grab the wheel if I do anything wrong."

"Out," Chris said again.

"Come on, Sue, let's get going," Matt said from in back.

In response, Sue sighed and slid back over on the passenger side again. Chris and Evie exchanged glances above the roof of the car. Then Evie got in back beside Matt, and Chris started the engine.

They headed southeast through Pisgah to Chapel Point, on narrow two-lane roads overhung with trees. Now and then there would be a break, a patch of sky, and the afternoon sun would cut through momentarily like the flash of a strobe light. Evie could feel Matt's eyes on her. She turned the other way.

St. Ignatius Church stood on a hilltop overlooking the junction of the Potomac and Port Tobacco Rivers.

"Oh, stop here a minute, Chris, I want you to see this!" Sue cried. "It's one of my favorite spots."

They all got out and walked through the churchyard toward the crest of the hill, looking down on the view below.

"Hey, this *is* something!" Chris said.

Bees buzzed deliciously amid the lush flowering shrubs, and the wind, skimming the top of the hill, stroked their faces.

For one brief moment the sun, the wind, and the delicate scent of roses made Evie forget about Sue, seemed to transport her far away, and it wasn't until Chris put his arm around her that she remembered. They stood together overlooking the valley, feeling like Indians, Chris said, who had probably stood on the same place once, looking down on the same rivers.

But to Evie, it seemed as though she could feel Sue's eyes like an arrow between the shoulder blades. When she turned finally, Sue was standing rigidly off by herself, staring out at the rivers in another direction, and Evie could tell that she knew.

When they all got in the car again, Sue hung back, forcing Evie to make the first move. And when Chris guided Evie to the front door and she got in, Sue climbed woodenly in back, a bunch of wild flowers drooping forlornly in her hand. Evie closed her eyes. It all seemed too cruel. She hated herself for her cowardice.

There was a place at Pope's Creek where the road came to a stop at the Potomac River. Two crab house restaurants squatted there along the water, their back sides hoisted up on long pilings, looking something like crabs themselves.

Chris parked, and they walked out on the pier. The Potomac was choppy, and the grayish waves lapped noisily against the posts. Far out on the water a boat glided cleanly by, its sail taut, its prow like the point of a compass as it skimmed the surface. The wind whipped their shirts, rocking the pier, and Evie paused, feeling giddy. Chris put his arm about her waist to steady her.

"Let's take the stuff over to the woods back there," said Matt. "Chris and Evie got to have their privacy." Evie glared at him furiously.

Coming around the car from opposite directions, the two girls met. It was as though Evie were looking at a stranger, for the eyes were like gray marbles, and the lips as straight as a ruler. Just the way Sue grabbed the blanket told all that needed saying.

Well, what will be will be, Evie told herself, trudging after her. It had all the makings of a soap opera—the mystery, the intrigue. . . . Will Sue forgive Evie? Will Evie change her mind about Chris? Will Chris become matchmaker for Sue and Matt? Will Matt ever open his mouth and say something tactful for a change?

For a while Evie pretended that nothing had happened—that they were all just friends out together on a Saturday afternoon. She did not hang around Chris but spread the blanket, distributed the plates, opened the relish. . . .

When the hamburgers were on and cooking, however, Chris rested his arm around Evie's shoulder again, and this time, as he talked, gently caressed her cheek with one thumb.

Evie felt the color rising in her face, and when she glanced at Sue finally, noticed the zombie-like way she was eating, eyes down, unsmiling. Oh lordy, Evie was thinking. What a mess! No wonder Rose preferred not to go out at all. How could something as simple as love get so complicated?

Chris, at least, seemed oblivious to the small drama going on about him. He ate the hamburger Sue didn't touch, and when Evie cut the cake, pulled out his ever-present drumsticks and gave a rolling fanfare on the lid of the relish jar. He didn't even notice that Sue had turned her back on them all.

He lay down on the blanket afterwards and pulled Evie down beside him.

"Look at that cloud," he said. "See that, Matt? What does it look like to you?"

"Charlie Brown's head," Matt ventured.

"A very pregnant mouse," said Evie.

"No, no, you've got the wrong one. Look. Right where I'm pointing. See that little projection on the right? That's Florida. Doesn't it look like a map of the states? What do you think, Sue?"

There was no answer.

"Hey, Sue!" Chris said again, good-naturedly. "Mooooody Sue! All of a sudden you're so quiet."

Evie lay tensely beside him, wishing there was some way she could shut him up. Were boys always like this—so obtuse?

"I'm going to the wharf and look around," Sue said in reply, and went down the path toward the river. Guilt gnawed away at Evie. So this was what it had been like for Rose and Donna Jean. She felt terrible.

The Chevy had to be back by seven, since Chris's father had a bowling match. They began to pack up at six-thirty.

"Sure seemed like a short picnic," Chris complained.

"Well, maybe next time we can stay longer," Evie

said, grateful to call an end to it. "There are a lot of places we could go. We'll make you love Maryland yet."

He smiled at her. "I already do."

Evie sat on the tombstone of Melvina Brice Laird, which had fallen over at an angle beneath Mr. Laird's upright gravestone. It formed a perfect chair.

She had been friends with Sue since seventh grade. They were as different as mustard and catsup, yet they liked each other and had always gotten along well. And now, the look on Sue's face. . . .

"Well, Evie, you found you a right good seat."

She jerked her head to see Frank Kettle coming across the grass, his boots caked with red clay, heading for the old tool shed beyond.

"I'm on my way home from a picnic," she told him. Because they were late getting back, she had told Chris to let her off at the end of the lane. Then she had taken refuge here, needing to sort things through.

Frank opened the door of the shed and stuck his shovel and pick inside. "Just dug me another grave. I told you there'd be more coming, didn't I?" He struck his boots against a gravestone to loosen the mud. "This one was for a man who wanted to be placed on top his brother's grave. I'm worryin' all the time that maybe the first grave hadn't been dug deep enough and my foot would go through. It happens sometimes."

"Why did he want to be buried on top?"

"Hard to figure what's in folks' minds when it comes to buryin'. Now if you ask me why the graves are pointin' the same way, I can tell you that."

Evie looked out over the rolling landscape and saw that, indeed, the graves were all angled more or less in the same direction.

"It's so the bodies can lie with their heads to the west, meaning they'll be facing east when the Last Judgment comes and they commence to sit up," Frank told her.

"I don't know," Evie said. "When I die, I think I'd rather be cremated and have my ashes scattered under a pear tree, so that people would think of me in the spring."

Frank Kettle nodded. "Yes, indeed, everybody wants himself remembered somehow. Most want a tombstone that's different, but then they go off and die and it's the folks left behind what does the decidin'." He pointed to a granite marker, sculpted like a broken column. "Now you see lots of them around—means an early death, a young man or woman cut off in the prime of life. If it's a lamb, it means a little child. See that anchor? No, over there a piece. Anchors mean fidelity, wheat sheaves resurrection, ivy eternal life—oh, there's a whole science to it, you know."

He began to smile more broadly now and sat down on a gravestone across from her, elbows resting on his knees, his grimy hands dangling loosely between his pant legs. "The strangest story I ever heard was one over in Calvert County, a man's wives fightin' over 'im. Fifteen, sixteen years ago, there was a big to-do when this man died, leaving his wife and the one he'd divorced before her. Well, when he was alive, the two women were stayin' up nights thinkin' up ways to torment the other, and after he died—kidneys, I think it was—they was even worse. Now this feller must not have been too smart to start with, because he bought himself three cemetery lots, thinking that would stop the fighting. When he died, see, he was to be buried in the middle, with a wife either side of him. At the funeral, don't you know, both of these women were carryin' on, each cryin' louder than the other. And the body weren't in the ground more'n three days but the wives was fightin' over who was to be buried on the right and who was to be on the left."

Evie began to smile, grateful for the distraction.

"The upshot was that the grave hadn't been dug too deep to start with, and it was on the side of a hill to boot. And that August, the tail end of a hurricane lashed through southern Maryland with a foot of water all over. The danged hill just caved in, and the man's casket went floatin' away and came to rest at the foot of an old sycamore, half-dead itself."

Frank's eyes began to water with merriment, and he pulled out a handkerchief and blew his nose. "Well, there was another big to-do over who was going to pay to have the casket buried again and the gravestone set up; and the cemetery allowed it didn't have the funds, that it was up to the kin. And don't you know, after all the squabblin' and cryin' and carryin' on, neither of those women wanted to claim 'im. Life sure is crazy."

"Love's crazier," Evie said. "Sometimes I think people would really like each other a lot if it weren't for love."

It rained on Sunday—a steady rain with neither lightning nor thunder, making a pond of bare places in the yard. The house had a musty smell of damp wood and dirty diapers that depressed Evie.

Tom was working quietly at the dining room table grading papers, and Donna Jean was cleaning out kitchen cupboards. As Evie sat on the couch, sorting the laundry, she tried to imagine what was going on in church that morning. There was something about people coming together to sing, flowers there at the altar, Mrs. Anderson's energetic playing of Bach, and the choir in their robes, rehearsed and ready, that made a celebration of even the worst sort of weather.

She had tried calling Sue that morning. There seemed to be some discussion in the background, and then Mrs. Shields said that Sue would call her back, but she didn't.

In a way that Evie could not explain, she blamed it all on Matt. Matt and his stupid remarks. Matt and his provocative questions. Here she was struggling so hard to walk the tightrope between her own family and the Rawleys, and Matt had to come along and throw her off-balance. Was she growing *away*, as Mother had worried? Would she, had she stayed at home, have encouraged Chris's attention without telling Sue? Was this the way godlessness began, trampling on somebody's feelings, or did things like this just happen?

She remembered years ago when a revival was going on in Branbury, and Matt had talked her into going. He had a way of talking her into things then, and she almost always got into trouble as a result. They sat in the back row, their feet scarcely touching the ground, and watched as the June bugs flew around and around the lights in the tent and the women fanned themselves with cardboard song sheets. They had giggled silently at the preacher who kept thumping his hand on the pulpit, and the woman who yelled "Yes, Jesus!" and the little old man, on Evie's right, who clapped in time to the music.

Then the preacher asked all those in need of God's forgiveness to come forward, and as Evie stared, almost everybody in the whole tent went to the altar except her and Matt. The preacher looked right at them and asked if there wasn't some small sin, some little dark spot, that needed forgiveness. Matt, still giggling, got down and crawled under the bench and back outside. It was Evie, her cheeks burning, who dutifully walked down the sawdust-strewn path to the front, where the preacher put his hand on her hand and said, "Bless you, sister."

Afterwards, when she got outside, Matt was rolling around on the grass, having a laughing fit, and Evie had gone home alone, ashamed and furious. She felt that way now.

The only bright spot in the dreariness was Joshua, who lay on a blanket on the floor, chortling with good feelings, kicking his legs and arms vigorously to some inner rhythm, smiling bubbles that were intercepted now and then by a crow of delight. Evie could not keep herself from him and knelt down to let her long hair brush back and forth across his face. This always startled him, made him blink, and then he would go into a frenzy of excitement, kicking and grunting, and Evie would laugh.

"You're going to give that kid a Lady Godiva complex," Tom said from the dining room. "He'll grow up with a fetish for long hair and probably run off with a cocktail waitress."

"No, he won't," Evie said, kissing Joshua's funny little nose. "He's never going to love anybody but me, are you, Josh?" And then, whispering in his ear, she added, "You're really mine, aren't you, love? I'll always believe you were sent to me."

The rain stopped early that afternoon, the sun came out, and clouds of steam rose from the water-logged ground. Evie watched the clock, but there was no call from Sue.

She sat on the porch swing beside the cat as rain dripped off the eaves, her journal on her lap: *A friend is a person with whom I may be sincere*, she had written. She was not sure who had said it— Emerson, she thought. And then she expressed her feelings in her own words:

It's not enough to be honest; I've got to be tactful as well, and no one's a worse example of that than Matt Jewell. If I had really told Sue in advance about Chris, would it have helped? And if I were in Sue's place, wouldn't I feel the same way? Trying to place the blame for a quarrel, though, only pro-longs it. . . .

Tom came to the screen. "What's up?"

"Nothing." She closed the book. "I'm thinking about becoming a hermit, that's all."

"Yeah?"

"Nobody to worry about but myself."

He came out on the porch, stretched, then sat down on the rail. "Well, I can recommend it for a while, anyway. When I was a bachelor, I didn't worry about anything, even myself. Summers I'd just hitchhike around the country if I felt like it— live out of a sleeping bag. And then, after I met

Donna Jean, I felt so responsible. I had someone I really cared about—someone to care *for*." He laughed. "I took out a life insurance policy and health insurance, and now that Josh is here, I'm already worrying about his college tuition. Can't have happiness without the worry, I guess." He studied her. "Something happen between you and Chris?"

"No. Sue and me."

"Oh." He waited, and when she said nothing more, asked. "How would you like some broiled bass for supper?"

"How can you think of supper when we just had lunch?"

"Easy. Come help me catch the bass."

"Go fishing?"

"Why not?"

As she changed into her old jeans, she heard voices coming from the yard, and her heart leaped. Perhaps Chris had come over. She went to the window. *Matt.* Her pulse slowed in disappointment. And when she got outside and heard Tom invite him to go along, she climbed in the back seat of the Dodge, amid the clutter of rods and reels, feeling irritable.

"Ever been fishing before, Matt?" Tom said as they went down the lane.

"Once, I guess. But I can't remember."

"Then how do you know you did?" Evie asked derisively.

There was a pause. "Well, Mom's got a picture

of me when I was real little—fishing with my dad."

Evie leaned back against the seat. Mean-spirited, that's what she was, but where Matt was concerned, she didn't much care.

Tom took back roads all the way, each one narrower than the last, until finally they were merely following tracks through a cow pasture. He parked.

Down the hill beyond the trees ran the Potomac. They walked to a sandy clearing where an old backless bench marked a popular fishing spot. Evie stood around half-heartedly while Tom and Matt untangled the lines.

"You want to bait your hook, Evie?" Tom said.

She didn't, but because Matt hesitated, she thrust her hand quickly down into the coffee can half-filled with dirt and gingerly picked up a fat gray worm. Watching Tom out of the corner of her eye, she stuck the worm over the hook, then looped it back again and thrust it over once more. She was surprised she did not throw up.

They cast off one at a time, each aiming for a separate place in the water. On the first throw, Evie's hook caught on a branch, and Matt climbed the tree to clear it. She should have thanked him, but she didn't.

Finally all the lines were in, the bobbers afloat. The glare on the water made her squint. There were only soft outdoor sounds—the buzz of insects, a bird call, the gentle sloshing of the current as foaming eddies washed up against the bank.

Evie was thinking of the way Aunt Ida always clicked her tongue when they drove to church and passed people fishing.

"A little prayer would do them more good than a catfish supper," she'd say.

And Evie's father would either say nothing at all or answer, "Mighty hard to pray on an empty stomach."

Tom caught a small fish, just big enough to keep, and put it in their bucket. They stood, and when their legs gave out, sat down on the bench, waiting. When an hour had gone by without another nibble, Tom pointed to some men fishing further down.

"I'm going to see if anything's biting," he said. "Keep an eye on my rod. Maybe we'll have to move."

"What do we do if there's a bite?" Evie called after him.

"Give the line a gentle jerk, and when it's taut, reel it in." He pushed on through the weeds.

"You heard from Sue?" Matt asked finally.

"No."

"Didn't think so."

"What's that supposed to mean?"

"Just figured the war was still on, that's all—you looking like you ate nails for breakfast."

"Well, I don't see that it's any of your business."

Matt braced his rod between his legs and rested his hands on the bench. "You know, you and your mother and Ida all have the same kind of face. You get teed off about something, you sort of bite your bottom lip. Ever notice how you do that?"

"No, I don't make a point of standing at the mirror all day."

Matt grinned. "I suppose not. That would be vanity. That's what your dad preached about this morning—vanity. He even hit the pulpit once with his fist. Big-time stuff!"

She looked at him. "You are really low, Matt Jewel! Sitting there making fun of my father and all the time living in his house."

"I wasn't making fun; I was making an observation."

"Well, I can do without your observations. You can just shut up and it will please me no end."

"What are you so touchy about? Your family so sacred I can't even talk about them?"

"Nothing *you* can say would hurt them, that's for sure."

"That's what I mean. What's the harm? I just think it's interesting the way your dad stands up there on Sunday morning and really cuts loose. Boy, he's a tiger in the pulpit, and at home he can hardly get a word in edgewise."

"Aunt Ida's always been bossy and talkative. It's just her nature."

"And your mom?"

She turned on him again. "My mother is the kindest, sweetest, most generous woman in the world,

Matt Jewel. She's delivered most all the babies in Charles County and never charged a cent." And then she added flippantly, "It wouldn't surprise me if she even delivered you, and why she didn't just drown you in the wash basin that very minute, I'll never know."

He gave a loud whistle. "Boy, you sure see things through rose-colored glasses, Evie. I swear you do. You ever notice the way she sits in that swing after Sunday dinner, with all the company gathered around her, like a queen with her court?" He raised his voice a little higher. " 'Oh, Ma Hutchins, these biscuits are the best.' 'I just don't see how you manage, Miz Hutchins, with two patients to tend to and Evie to raise.' 'Mrs. Hutchins, I sure do thank you for your generosity.' And all the while poor old Murphy's trotting back and forth to fetch this and that like some old man-servant, with Rose and Ida. . . ."

At that instant the bobber on Matt's line went under. As he jerked to grab his rod, he lost his balance and tumbled backwards, the rod slipping out from between his knees.

Evie shrieked gleefully as he lunged after it, scrambling across the ground, and then she saw her own bobber go under. The line went taut.

"I got something!" she yelled. The line relaxed, then grew tight once more, and she remembered to give it a quick jerk. It began moving through the water and the rod bent slightly at the end.

"Pull it in! Pull it in!" yelled Matt.

Down the bank, Evie could see Tom running toward them. She began reeling in as fast as she could, but lost her grip and the line spun out. Frantically she clamped one hand on it and tried again, reeling rapidly until she felt the line tighten—heavy. The rod bent a little more.

The next thing she knew, the line rose up out of the water with a foot-long fish flopping about on the end, and she was screaming, "I got one! I got one!"

Tom arrived in time to help get it off the hook, while Matt discovered that his had got away. Evie rode home happy. Even when Matt told her she had sounded like Sue Shields, the way she carried on, it didn't bother her. Matt Jewel wasn't worth the powder to blow him to hell. He'd get there soon enough on his own.

If there was a hell.

Ten

SUE HAD NOT PHONED while she was gone.

Evie gamely helped Tom and Matt scale the fish on a stump in the back yard. Matt, of course, was invited to stay for supper. The yellow stray climbed up on the window ledge outside and meowed.

"Yond Cassius has a lean and hungry look," Tom said. "Give him the leftovers, Donna Jean. He looks as if he could use a little love."

As soon as the meal was over, Evie went upstairs for a long bath, vowing to stay there until she heard Matt leave. She washed her hair, trimmed her nails, and at long last—just before dusk—heard the squeak of the bicycle and saw him riding away. Good riddance.

Later, when she helped put the dishes away and swept up, she went out by herself to walk. The cat followed her halfway down the lane to the highway and then, perhaps bored by her inattention, let her continue the rest of the way alone.

Everything she had ever believed, she felt, was suddenly up for grabs. How do you grow up without growing away? And if that was not possible, how do you grow away without tearing everyone apart?

Her hair felt silky as the wind blew it across her face. She liked the smell of clean hair and camphor and the earth after a summer rain. And honeysuckle.

She stopped as she came abreast of the cemetery, and her nostrils picked up the scent of the delicate flower. And then, with a rush, she remembered Chris and how they had stopped that first night on the lane, listening to a mockingbird. If only she had said something to him then about Sue. . . .

Evie had just started back when she heard footsteps and turned around. She could tell by the walk and the height and finally, the shock of white-blond hair, that it was Chris. She had thought he might come. Evie moved toward him, and he held out his arms.

She was warm with her happiness. Had she ever experienced such a moment as this, such a heady feeling of contentment? When at last she raised her face to look at him, he bent and kissed her on the lips as she had wanted. So this was what it was like the day that Tom had come for Donna Jean, when Donna Jean could have thought of Rose but didn't. She determined to say it quickly and get it over with.

"Chris, I think Sue was hurt yesterday." Her arms were around his neck. "She likes you very much. I guess it was a shock for her to see us together."

He stared at her, surprised, then laughed and rubbed his nose against hers. "I didn't know I was so popular."

"I really mean it. I tried to call her this morning, but she wouldn't talk to me."

He held her out a little way from him so that he could see her face. "I never encouraged her, did I?"

"Well, I don't know, exactly. Maybe she just had her hopes up."

"I'm sorry, then. I didn't mean to hurt her. But I'd feel worse if I ever hurt you."

And then they kissed again, so long, so tenderly, that all thoughts of Sue slipped away. They walked back and forth along the lane, so many times that they lost count, stopping now and then to hug, rocking softly together. Donna Jean came to the screen once as they neared the porch, looked out, then moved away and did not come to the door again. How wonderful it was being in love here at the Rawleys—the freedom, the privacy. . . . She could not quite picture the same scene on the driveway back home.

Five weeks old. Joshua was looking more like a baby every day, less like an infant, and was fast outgrowing the basket in which he slept. The scrawny arms with the skin hanging loose had become chubby, the legs creased with little scallops of fat. When Evie changed him, he would stare perplexed at the ceiling when she disappeared from view, then smile and thrash his arms and legs when she popped up again. Peek-a-boo was almost more than his nervous system could bear. The little knit shirts that had seemed to swallow him up as a newborn now stretched tightly over his expanding chest and tummy, and when he was dry and powdered, he would coo with such obvious delight that Evie would gather him up in her arms, nuzzling his ear. *Josh, I do love you so!*

The K-Mart was having a sale on cribs, and Donna Jean and Tom wanted to look them over. Evie and Joshua went along for the ride. Inside the store, Evie pushed the stroller around, circling the candy counter with its fragrant aroma of maple clusters and bridge mix, on past stationery and greeting cards toward housewares. Joshua would fix his eyes on a bright spot of color—a flashing sign above the record counter or a pinwheel of colored towels above linens—and crow his approval.

It was just beyond the shoe department that they met—Evie and Sue.

Evie stopped. "Hi, Sue."

"Hi." The voice was flat, restrained.

Evie half expected her to move on, but when she didn't, Evie said, "Donna Jean and Tom are looking at cribs. You shopping?"

"With Mother. She's trying on dresses."

It seemed to Evie that something was called for at this point, some word of friendship: "What have you been doing lately? You haven't been by." They started walking slowly down the wide aisle.

"Why should I?" Sue said, not looking at her.

Evie chanced it. "I thought we were friends."

"So did I. Until the picnic."

It was a relief to have it out. "I haven't changed how I feel about you, Sue."

"Why should you? *I* didn't do anything to hurt *you.*"

"Tell me what you would have done in my place."

"Well, nobody ever accused me of seeing someone's boyfriend behind her back."

"I didn't know he belonged to you."

"You knew I liked him."

"Yes, but so did I. You never asked me that."

"So you just moved in and took over."

"Chris has been coming by. I didn't ask him to. Sometimes things just happen."

They walked on together for a while, quietly, but Sue made no move to leave.

"Well," she said finally, "it seems the least you could have done was call and tell me."

"I thought of it, and I should have, but I just didn't know what to say. If I'd told you Chris liked me, would it have made you feel any better?"

"It would have kept me from making a fool of

myself. I can imagine what Chris thinks of me now, sitting up there by him in the front seat."

"Listen, Sue, there's not a boy in the world who wouldn't be flattered to have *ten* girls sitting by him in the front seat. The only thing you did was make Chris have an exceptionally good time."

They both smiled a little at that.

"It could have been the other way around," Evie said as they made a full circle and started back again. "If we're going to get mad at each other every time a boy looks at us, we might as well just shoot ourselves and get it over with."

"Well, I don't want to be taken by surprise, Evie. If there's something I should know, don't wait and tell me last."

"I'm sorry it happened this way. It was all just so awkward."

Finally Sue said, "I guess it would be pretty ridiculous to go the rest of the summer without speaking. I'll call you in a day or two when I get my head together."

"I'm glad. It wouldn't seem like summer without you."

When Evie went to Hollander's on Friday, Chris was sitting on the porch with a sandwich and a bag of Fritos.

"Want some?" He held out the bag toward her.

"No, I just fed Josh some strained cereal and I lost my appetite."

"He didn't like it?"

"He sneezed."

They laughed.

"Guess what? I got my new Zildjian ride cymbal."

"You did? Is it your birthday?"

"Not till September, but someone was having a sale, so Dad bought it for me early. Listen, I've got forty minutes left in my lunch hour. You want to see it? I'll play something for you."

"Sure."

Chris bounded up on the porch. "I'll be back by one-thirty, Mr. Hollander," he called through the screen, and they set off across the field toward a side street.

Evie had no idea where Chris lived—what his house or even his father looked like. When she thought of him in fantasy, she remembered the way he looked in the dusk there on the lane, his hair silhouetted against the moon. It was strange thinking of him in any other setting—getting up in the morning, having breakfast, scrubbing the sink. . . .

It was a small shingled box of a house, very much like the ones on either side of it, with a chain link fence and a tree so large it completely overshadowed the roof. There was no car in the drive.

Chris unlocked the door. The house had a closed-up smell of bacon and stale bedding. Here and there a stray sock or a jacket lay on a chair— what one might expect, Evie decided, from a working father and his teenage son.

Chris led her back to his room.

"There!" he said proudly.

There was scarcely space for anything but the drum set and the bed. Shining black drums mottled with silver sat grouped together at various heights, with cymbals and stands. An array of sticks covered the dresser top.

"Wow!" Evie said admiringly.

"It's a Ludwig set," Chris told her, running one finger over the rim of the snare. "And this is the new Zildjian.' He picked up a drumstick from his dresser and struck the metal disk sharply on the top, then again, cocking his head at the sound, listening acutely. "Hear that? Hear the ping?" He struck it again. "See how long it goes on—how clear?" He smiled broadly. "Isn't it neat?"

"It's beautiful. They're all so beautiful."

"Oh, you should see some of the drums they make now—transparent heads, mahogany veneer, drums that are lighted up all around on the inside. But that's big money. Go on, sit down. I'll play something for you."

He took his seat on the padded stool in the middle of the drums, and Evie sat on the bed. For just a minute he paused, sticks in hand, then began a slow *rat-a-tat-tat* on the snare, to the beat of the bass, gradually increasing the tempo until his hands became a blur. From snare to tom-toms he moved, one after another—the tone becoming higher or lower.

The high-hat cymbals parted and clanged together again as Chris worked the pedal, adding a syncopated beat to the thump of the bass. Now and then the huge cymbal, the beautiful golden Zildjian, pinged out a clear note above the hypnotic beat of the snare. Faster and faster the tempo moved until even the assortment of sticks on the dresser was vibrating.

It was a new experience, an overwhelming sound. But above the noise and the clamor, Evie could sense that Chris was indeed gifted. It was a coolly polished performance of restraint and precision.

"Chris," she said honestly when the number was over. "You really *are* good."

He grinned with pleasure. "You didn't know before?"

"Well, it's certainly a lot different from hearing you play on Crisco cans."

He laughed. "I worked out a new arrangement last night of that song that's been playing on WWDC. Want to hear it?"

"Sure."

Again the hands moved deftly above the snare, then above the three tom-toms, and the sneakered foot on the bass pedal moved inconspicuously up and down, the rhythm a strange combination of jazz and rock. Evie clapped enthusiastically when he had finished, and Chris blushed a little, put down his sticks, and came over. He pulled out a catalogue

159

from the bottom drawer of his dresser and sat down beside her, thumbing through it.

"Here's the set I'd like to have some day. Named after Buddy Rich." He pointed to an eight-piece drum set of white marine pearl.

"It's gorgeous," said Evie, "but you can only play a couple drums at a time anyway. What's the point of so many?"

He laughed and put one arm about her shoulder. "All the drums are different. See these? These are the tom-toms. You can get all different sizes and they each give a different sound."

They continued turning the pages, commenting on one drum set, then another. After a while they grew silent and just looked at the pictures, and then Evie could tell that Chris was watching her, not the catalogue. She turned to him and let the book slide off her lap as he bent to kiss her, encircling her with both arms.

There was something different about being here in this room with Chris, being alone together in his house—not unpleasant, just new. Out on the lane near the Rawleys', with the sky and trees about them, Evie had somehow felt more protected than she did here. Yet she loved the feel of his lips, the stroke of his hands. They leaned nearer the bed and lay down, holding each other closely.

For a moment Evie felt as though she were suffocating, for her breath almost stopped. Her heart pounded loudly, a violent thumping that she was sure Chris could feel through his shirt. Yet she clung to him, relishing his kiss, the feel of his hands about her shoulders, her sides. And then she felt his hardness against her groin. For a moment they continued lying there as a new sensation, more urgent, radiated through her, along her inner thighs. And suddenly Chris sat up.

"I guess we'd better go, Evie," he said, standing. "I . . . didn't mean to put you on the spot."

They went slowly back to the grocery, arms about each other, her head against his shoulder. Things had gone as far as they would let them, but she knew now what she had always suspected, that sex was something she would enjoy. She looked up at Chris and smiled, and he kissed her lightly on the forehead, the way he had done that first night. And then they were at Hollander's and he kissed her again before going inside.

"I love your drums, Chris," she told him.

He held her fingers a moment. "I love you," he said.

As the screen closed after him and Evie started down the steps, her head fairly bursting with joy, she saw Rose sitting in her car on the edge of the parking lot, in the shade.

"Well!" Rose said, stepping out. "I thought this was a public place."

Evie didn't answer. Rose closed the car door and came over.

"Donna Jean know you're up here with that boy?"

"Of course she knows I'm here. That's Chris Lundgren."

"Well, at least you know his name. Nobody I ever saw before."

"He's in Branbury for the summer. He works here at Hollander's."

"Oh." Rose shifted her purse to her other arm. "Sure doesn't look much like work to me."

"Oh, for heaven's sake, Rose."

"Well, I swear, Evie, it's getting so I never know what I'm going to see anymore on my lunch hour. The girls at the bank all lie out on the grass, the men practically on top of them. And then I stop by here and find you kissing right out by the highway. Might as well put up a sign and advertise yourself."

"What on earth are you talking about?" Evie snapped. "You sound like Aunt Ida. *Worse* than Aunt Ida! You keep yourself all shut up away from people, and then you can't stand it when somebody else falls in love. . . ." She stopped, her chest heaving.

"Evie!" Rose said, her mouth contorted. "After all I've been through . . . !"

"So you've been hurt!" Evie said. "Well, you're going to go on being disappointed, Rose, if you keep backing away from love. You'll ruin your whole life just because you didn't get the man you had your heart set on, but I won't let you ruin mine!"

And then Mr. Hollander was at the screen. "Well,

well, Rose—come in. Thought I heard you out here. Haven't seen you for a good long spell." And Evie walked swiftly back down the highway toward Donna Jean's, her legs shaking, her breath coming fast.

It needed to be said, she told herself. Someone had to say it. All these years, Rose had been afraid to take another chance. How did you grow at all—or love or leave home—if you didn't take chances?

There was a phone call for Evie after dinner. Thinking it was Chris, she stretched the cord around the corner of the kitchen and sat in the hallway, cradling the receiver in her hands.

"Hello," she said softly. Her mood crumbled when she heard her mother's voice.

"Hello, dear. How are things going?"

"Oh, fine!" Evie tried to sound lighthearted. "We just finished dinner, and I was about to help Donna Jean with the dishes."

"Well, I won't keep you long, then. I certainly do hope you're being a help to her. She must have so much to do these days."

The caution between them was growing.

"Of course I am, Mother."

"And you haven't forgotten your promise to come back for a Saturday in August and help out when we put up the preserves?"

"I'll be back." This was not what her mother had called about at all.

"I was wondering," said Mrs. Hutchins, "just how much you've been seeing that boy at Hollander's."

"I knew it! Rose has been at it again."

There was a pause. "Rose has nothing to do with this, Evie."

"Then what is it?"

The sky was perfectly clear beyond the screen, yet it seemed to Evie that storm clouds were gathering above the line of trees.

"I had a somewhat disturbing phone call this afternoon. I'm not going to mention any names, but it was a neighbor of the Lundgrens'. She told me that you and Chris spent some time in his house today while his father was at work. Now you know how that looks, Evie. . . ."

Oh, Lord, they sure didn't need newspapers in Branbury. Anything that happened in this place was broadcast over the wires in a space of three minutes.

"We did, Mother. He just got a new cymbal for his drums and wanted to show it to me."

There was silence. Then, "She said you were in there for quite some time, dear."

"He played the drums, Mother! Didn't Miss Know-It-All even hear them? Anybody within three blocks would have heard those drums."

Was it possible, Evie wondered, for her mother to detect a half-truth? Or was it a lie? Was it necessary at sixteen to confess everything to your mother, especially when you had shown such commendable restraint?

"Well," Mrs. Hutchins said quickly, "I know that I can trust you, Evie. But remember how it looks, especially to our church folk, and you the minister's daughter. I really don't want you to go there again unless his father is home. People do talk."

"I guess they do." *Small-town people! Small-town minds!*

Eleven

SUMMER TOOK ON A NEW MOOD, as though the
curtain had dropped, the scene had changed, and
the players had put on new costumes. The four of
them—Evie, Chris, Matt, and Sue—gathered each
evening at the Rawley's. Their relationship had an
air of innocence, and they seemed to delight in a
return to foolishness and laughter. Now that Evie
and Chris were officially "going together," the at-
mosphere was more relaxed. Sue seemed more natural, Matt more resigned.

With Donna Jean watching from the porch,
Joshua on her lap, someone would begin a game of
touch football. Sometimes Tom would put aside his
lesson plans and come out to join them—sprinting
across the clearing, the ball beneath his arm, dodg-
ing the hands that tried to clutch him, and Donna
Jean would shriek her encouragement.

After Sue and Matt left, Chris would begin his sweet, prolonged goodbye. He and Evie would sit on the swing, the light from the window illuminating only one small patch of the porch, catching the tips of their feet, leaving the rest of them in darkness. They would rock, the slow squeak of the chain an accompaniment to their whispers. And then Evie would walk halfway down the lane to the road with him, drinking in the smell of his skin, his shirt, his hair.

Other times the gathering took place in midafternoon at Hollander's, when business was slow, with a summer storm, perhaps, threatening off in the southwest. As the dark clouds came closer, bringing with them a damp smell of earth, the four would stand out on the gravel parking lot and throw Frisbees, Mr. Hollander watching from the porch. Even when the first raindrops hit, they would laugh and taunt the sky and, when the deluge came, make a run for the steps.

"Nuthin' in the *world* I like better'n a summer rain," Hollander would always say, hands folded on his belly, rocking in the old metal chair as millions of raindrops danced noisily on the tin roof overhead.

Most afternoons, however, Evie and Donna Jean worked in their shop. The floor of the study had been covered with newspapers, which were layered in turn with specks of paint and wood shavings. The shelves had been painted, and only the counters were yet to be made.

On this particular afternoon, Evie and Donna Jean bent over a large piece of plywood, which was to be the sign above the front door. They had carefully mapped out in large letters, "The Cousins," and now began filling in the letters with paint, each to be done like a sample of fabric—one letter striped, another checked, another dotted with flowers.

"The day this sign goes up, I'm going to scream with happiness," Evie declared, as she dipped her small brush in the blue and colored in the "e."

Donna Jean sat up on her knees. "No, you won't. We've talked about it so long and worked so hard that we'll hardly even notice." She sighed. "All we've got to sell so far are the things we've made ourselves. No way in the world we're going to have time to travel around and find things on consignment before Christmas." She shook her head. "Sometimes I think I must be crazy to believe this will really work. Other times I think, well, what if it doesn't? At least I've got Tom and Josh."

Joshua seemed to know that he was being talked about because he babbled at them from his infant seat across the floor, blowing little bubbles of spit, his eyes focused on a beam of sunshine coming through the window.

Donna Jean crawled over the newspapers to her baby. Leaning over him, her face seemed a polka-dot fabric all its own, the faint tan freckles contrasting sharply with the clear pink of Joshua's skin.

"Hi, old buddy," she said softly, holding out a finger for him to grasp. "What do you think—are the cousins going to make it or not?"

Joshua tilted his face upwards, captivated by hers, his mouth working vigorously, eyes smiling, cooing out a welcome.

She swept him up in her arms and held him high above her, little feet dangling, then brought him down and hugged him hard. "Oh, Evie, if I ever believed there was a God, it's when I hold this baby. I never had a more wonderful gift in my life."

Perhaps, because Joshua was seven weeks old, or because he was now sleeping through the night and Donna Jean felt more rested, she accepted a telephone invitation from Evie's mother to dinner on Sunday. And in the spirit of the occasion, much to Evie's astonishment, Tom suggested that they should attend church first, taking the baby with them.

"I'm just vain enough I want everybody to see him," Donna Jean agreed as she slipped on her good dress.

"You going to behave yourself, Senator?" Tom asked Josh, carrying the infant seat to the car. The baby hiccuped and smiled at no one in particular.

It was Evie, now, who had reservations about going. In the past few weeks she had come to feel a real part of her new household, closer to them at times than she felt to her own family. She had always hoped they would return to church and come back to the old house for dinner, but now she did not relish being scrutinized by Rose or lectured to by Aunt Ida, or—worse yet—left face to face with her mother. She had nothing to report, she had made no converts, and she herself was in turmoil. As for her father. . . . What if she ended up like Matt, not believing anything? What if, no matter how hard she tried, there were always doubts?

She would have liked to carry Josh in herself, but when they parked outside the little stucco church, it was Tom who lifted the infant seat and carried it proudly up the steps.

Things were just as Evie knew they would be. She could have written the script:

"Donna Jean, how good to see you!"

"So this is the baby, Lord bless him!"

"We're mighty glad to have you, Tom. Know you're right proud of that boy."

Slowly, slowly they moved down the aisle as hands reached out to pat Joshua's arm or tweak his foot. Settled at last, Tom spread a clean diaper over one shoulder and held Joshua up, the blue eyes of the baby staring shamelessly at the delighted people behind.

Rose and Aunt Ida had stayed home this time, and it was Mrs. Hutchins and Matt who joined the Rawleys in the pew.

"What if Josh pukes or something?" Matt whispered.

"Oh, shut up," Evie said disgustedly. Leave it to Matt to say something stupid.

The music of the morning was Haydn, not Bach, according to the mimeographed program. There seemed to Evie just as many curliques to it, and it kept Mrs. Anderson's hands just as busy, but it was gayer somehow, more dancelike, less like music for church.

During the announcements that followed, Mr. Hutchins welcomed the Rawleys:

"We have a very special guest with us today, and seeing as how he's not paying a bit of attention, I'm going to ask his father to stand up and show him off—Joshua John Rawley, seven weeks old."

Tom smiled as he stood up, Joshua's little red head bobbing about on his shoulder.

"Welcome Tom and Donna Jean, and your little son," Evie's father said, and voices called out, "God bless you all."

Evie began to feel again the warm nurturing and love that she had always received from this congregation and it calmed her. Did Tom and Donna Jean feel any of it? she wondered. Once you got to be an "outsider," was it hard to recapture again? Or would it always be so easy to slip back into the quiet acceptance she had always felt in this place?

The sermon was not about prodigals.

"I'll never forget my first pair of ice skates," Mr. Hutchins said, and this—in the heat of an early August morning—brought on a ripple of laughter.

"With wobbly legs and wavering ankles, I started across the pond, clutching at the air as my torso tipped forward, then back. When I fell, a crashing blow against the unforgiving ice, I saw stars—millions of stars—floating, circling, spiraling about the darkness inside my head." It was a good beginning, Evie thought, until she remembered that her father, growing up in Georgia, had probably never been on ice skates at all.

It turned out to be a sermon on the cosmos—about how an ant, when it reaches your foot there in the grass, only senses that something huge is present. It does not know about you or even what a person is. It knows nothing of factories or music or philosophy or international affairs. Its world is very small, perhaps only a piece of a meadow or a sandlot. And so are we to God, mere ants in our knowledge of the universe, ignorant of space and things far too vast for our comprehension.

Evie listened intently. It was a sermon that her father must have worked on for a long time. She knew by his choice of words and the careful way he read certain sections that he wanted it to be one of his best. And yet she was unsatisfied when it ended, feeling no real conclusion within herself.

A Christian who has not received the Holy Ghost

is like a house that has been wired for electricity, but the power has never been turned on—one of Aunt Ida's favorite sayings. Obviously, her aunt would say, the problem lay with Evie.

Except for a brief visit with the Hutchinses after her honeymoon, Donna Jean had not been back inside the house that had once been her home.

And not once, Evie was thinking as they turned up the winding drive, had the family ever discussed it—as though a remark, a word, even, could hurt Rose more than she could bear. Treated like a fragile flower, Rose had become more fragile still.

Murphy was standing under the beech tree, shading his eyes with his hand, watching for them. Then he turned and hurried excitedly into the house.

The moment the car stopped, Joshua was passed from one admiring relative to the next, his eyes heavy with sleep, his mood cranky.

"Bless his little heart!" Aunt Ida clucked, kissing him on the cheek. "Just gettin' his little self not one bit of rest!"

But when it came Rose's turn to take him, she remembered a salad that needed dressing and retreated at once to the kitchen, avoiding Evie's eyes.

Mrs. Hutchins spread out an old blanket on the couch in the living room for Josh, pushing chairs against it to keep him from rolling off. Donna Jean sat down to nurse him back to sleep.

"You just take all the time you need now, Donna Jean—my goodness, him being passed around like a sack of sugar—and then we'll eat. Not a thing that can't wait, so don't you feel rushed." Mrs. Hutchins turned to Evie. "We're eating in the kitchen this time, and Sister Ozzie's joining us. You won't believe her appetite these days—such an improvement! I do think it's Matt. She likes having a young man about. Let's see, I left Mr. Schmidt with his pudding dish. Would you get it? Then we'll see about some extra chairs. . . ."

The hurry, the bustle, the chain of command—how obvious it all seemed to Evie now. The familiar sounds, the requests, the suggestions seemed especially irksome, as though her ears had become unusually sensitive. There was the familiar clatter from the kitchen, the shuffle of chairs, the frenetic jabber of several people all talking at once, and over it all, the loud plaintive wail of Sister Ozzie from the back bedroom, claiming that she had been forgotten. Evie longed for the quiet of the Rawleys' house, dismayed that she found her homecoming so irritating.

Mr. Schmidt seemed to sense that there was company about, for he was listening intently, his hands clutching the pudding dish. The spoon had rolled onto the sheet and left a tapioca stain.

"Hello," Evie said warily, walking around the bed. "It's good to see you again. Do you remember me?"

He looked at her, his heavy black brows knotted together in concentration. Somehow the eyes did not seem as fierce as she had remembered them— merely puzzled. He cocked his head as Josh gave a sleepy bleat from the next room.

"We brought a baby along," Evie explained, reaching slowly for the pudding dish. "He's going to sleep now, but when he wakes up I'll bring him in and let you see him."

Her fingers closed around the edge of the bowl, but Mr. Schmidt held on.

"Mother asked me to come for your bowl. Let me have it, and I'll bring you a cookie. Would you like that?"

The brows knotted together even closer, and the old gnarled fingers clasped the dish so tightly that the knuckles showed white.

The door from the pantry opened, and Matt came in. Evie felt embarrassed at her ineptness.

"Give me the bowl," she demanded sternly of the old man.

Matt came up behind her. "I'll take care of it, Evie," he said, and went around the bed to the window, raising the blind a little. He pointed to Tom's car.

"Do you see that old Dodge?" he asked Mr. Schmidt. "My grandfather used to have a really old one with a running board and fenders."

Mr. Schmidt leaned forward and peered out the window.

"Did you ever have a car with a running board?" Matt asked him. "Or a rumble seat, maybe?"

The old man smiled faintly. Evie stared.

"Well, that's Tom Rawley's car. It's not *that* old, but it's old." Matt picked up a tray on the side table and held it out, and Mr. Schmidt placed his bowl on it, then the spoon. "When we're through with dinner, I'm going to ask Tom if he'll take you for a ride. I think you'd enjoy it."

Mr. Schmidt smiled, a full smile this time. It was the first time Evie remembered him smiling. He understood far more than she had ever imagined. For three years they had assumed that his mind was as full of gibberish as the nonsense words he spoke, when he chose to speak at all. She turned quickly, preceding Matt from the room.

Everyone was at the table when Donna Jean finally came in from the living room.

"Josh has been wakened so many times this morning that he's fussy, but I think he'll sleep now," she said, sliding into her chair.

"Goodness, Donna Jean, you don't need to apologize for putting a child to bed!" Aunt Ida said, hugging her. "That fried chicken isn't going to get up and walk away. You just eat a nice slow meal, now, and the young one will see to himself."

"I've rocked more babies myself than I can count," Mrs. Hutchins said, and then, nodding toward her husband, bowed her head for the blessing.

Mr. Hutchins sat with his fingers on the edge

176

of the table, his eyes tightly shut, face turned upwards.

"I want the mashed potatoes, please," came Sister Ozzie's voice.

"Hush," said Rose.

"Our Heavenly Father," Mr. Hutchins began, "you do indeed give us wondrous blessings, and one of the greatest of these is friendship. Whenever there is a new life among us, we are all a thousand times blest, and we thank you in particular for the gift of Joshua John. May we be humbled by the innocence of this child and may he, in turn, be inspired by us, so that—like Christ in the temple— he will grow in wisdom and stature and favor with God and man. Amen."

"Amen," said Mrs. Hutchins.

"Amen," said Murphy, from his end of the table.

"I want the mashed potatoes, please," Sister Ozzie said again in a loud petulant voice. She was staring at Evie as though she had never seen her before, with rouge the size of half dollars on either cheek. She seemed to be wearing every necklace she owned.

"You shall have some, my dear, with a little forbearance," Mother told her.

"For you, Madam," Tom said graciously, holding the bowl so that Sister Ozzie could help herself. She stared at him too, then giggled.

Rose was sitting about as far down the table from Tom and Donna Jean as she could get, carrying on a running conversation with Murphy. Every time Murphy lifted his fork to his mouth, Evie noticed, it seemed there was another question waiting to be answered.

"How's the teaching going, Tom?" Father asked. "How do you take to summer school?"

"Well, there are other things I'd rather be doing when it's hot, but I'm teaching a special science program for gifted students. I enjoy it—I'm glad for the challenge. That's why I found your sermon so interesting—the analogy of the ant. I'd like to use it in class as an example of how little we really know about the universe."

"I'd be flattered."

"The gravy, please! I would like the gravy!" Sister Ozzie was insistent.

"That woman!" said Rose.

"Be patient, Sister Ozzie," Aunt Ida told her. "Murphy, that gravy's sitting there by your elbow. Now you mind and keep things going around."

"Get that extra pitcher of iced tea from the porch, would you, Murphy?" Mrs. Hutchins said.

The hired man quickly pushed back from the table, jiggling the glasses.

"Murphy, I declare!" Rose said. "*Watch* yourself."

Evie lifted her eyes and found herself looking again at Matt. Everything he had said about her family was true. How was it possible she had lived so long in this house and never noticed?

"How are things going at the bank, Rose?"

It was strange how so ordinary a question could seemingly cut through the room like electricity. There was a second or two of awkward silence, as though Tom should not have asked, the old connection not have been made.

Rose flushed and lifted her water glass, and Mrs. Hutchins answered for her, "Oh, she's busy as usual. Since they put in the new drive-in window, she's working Saturday mornings, too."

"Is that right?" Tom said, and looked at Rose.

But she got up suddenly, saying, "The rolls!" and fussed about the oven.

For a few moments it seemed as though everyone felt the tension. And then it was Matt's voice that broke the silence: "I liked the story about the ant, too," he said, returning to Mr. Hutchins' sermon, "but the problem is it didn't answer anything."

Now all motion at the table ceased in earnest—all chewing, all cutting—and eyes turned toward the square-faced boy across from Evie.

Mr. Hutchins put down his fork. "What in particular, Matt?"

"Well, if there's a lot out there we don't know anything about, how do we know it's even God?"

Aunt Ida's hand dropped to her lap, and she leaned forward and peered down the table at Matt.

"Because I believe the Bible," Mr. Hutchins said simply, and began quoting a favorite verse: " 'For now we see through a glass, darkly; but then face to face; now I know in part; but then shall I know even as also, I am known.' Because I feel the power of Jesus in my own life, and I've seen what He can do."

Evie glanced around. Both Tom and Donna Jean had resumed eating, but no one else.

"A roll!" Ozzie said. "I didn't get a roll."

Rose picked up the basket and fairly thrust it at her.

Matt sat looking at his thumb nail. "What can He do?" he asked finally. "Jesus, I mean?"

"Why, Matt Jewel, do you never read the Bible?" Aunt Ida was indignant. "The lame to walk? The deaf to hear? The dumb to speak?"

Murphy had stopped halfway across the kitchen floor on one of his errands and stood frozen in his tracks at the nerve of Matt Jewel.

"Why, the wonders we've seen right in our own congregation!" put in Mother. "When Sally Nicholson was sick last year—remember, Rose?—and the doctors almost gave up on her, the whole congregation prayed, and she got better. Now that was a miracle. God can do wondrous, wondrous things."

"But what about the ones who don't get better?" Matt asked earnestly. "What about when the whole congregation gets down on their knees, and the person goes ahead and dies?"

"Matt Jewel!" cried Aunt Ida. "Why, your mother would be ashamed!"

"He can't even ask?" Tom said gently.

"It's not our place to question," Evie's mother said. "That's exactly what Mr. Hutchins was saying in his sermon—that God is so vast, so complex, that we can't understand His plan for us."

Why didn't her father speak for himself, Evie wondered. Why did he just sit there and let the women do the talking? She implored him with her eyes.

"Is it a plan, then?" The voice this time was Donna Jean's. It was a soft voice, but there was a slight tremor to it. "Was it God's plan that my mother be killed in that car accident? Was He responsible for that?"

Aunt Ida turned slowly and gaped at Donna Jean.

"You see," Matt cut in, "if God helps sometimes but not others, then He *could* do something about evil in the world, but He doesn't."

"Well, I never!" Aunt Ida pushed her chair back. "I never thought I would hear such talk at this table in the presence of a man of God!"

"Ida, be quiet."

It was Father, finally. His eyes were stern, and he stared at his sister-in-law, who finally picked up her napkin and dabbed at her mouth.

"God didn't give us brains to sit on, and Matt's at least trying to use his." He looked over at Tom and Donna Jean. "I don't have the answers for anyone but myself. I certainly don't believe that God wanted your mother to die in that accident, Donna Jean, or even that He let it happen. Why she wasn't saved, I don't know. For me, I don't need the answer in order to worship Him. I feel His presence in my life, and that's enough."

"But how do you know it's Him?" Matt insisted earnestly. "Some people feel great when they climb mountains. Some people feel it when they jog. Some say it's music or meditation or yoga that does it. How can you be sure it's God?"

"Because that's what it seems to me," Mr. Hutchins said. "It's my hope that one day you'll feel it too; but meanwhile, I won't have anyone at my table. . . ." He turned his head, taking in Mother and Rose too, "looking down on someone while he's working it through. We're all of us on that journey. There's not a soul in this room who's gone as far as he could."

Slowly the eating resumed. The platter of chicken went around again and then the peas. Murphy fetched the tea pitcher a second time and filled the glasses. This time Mother remembered to thank him. Forks resumed their familiar clink against the plates, and Aunt Ida rose finally to get the dessert.

"It's a beautiful day for cherry pie," said Sister Ozzie.

Twelve

EVIE SAT ON THE TOMBSTONE, her head against a tree. Frank Kettle was nearby, straightening fallen markers, digging deep slots for them in the soft earth. He seemed to sense her need for solitude, and let her be.

She hardly felt the cold of the marble beneath her, did not smell the flowers, heard no hum of bees. She was numb to everything except the pulse of her own heart as it sent the blood seething through her.

She was overwhelmed with an inexplicable rage toward Matt. All of the animosity toward him that had been building up over the weeks came spurting out now, no more reasonable than it had been before, but far more distinct. It was almost something she could touch. The very nearness of it alarmed her.

How dare he? No matter how circuitous the route

her logic took, it always came back to that. For once she sided with Aunt Ida in her indignation. How dare he turn on them like that in their own house, at their own table!

The rest of the meal had gone almost ludicrously well. The dessert had been served with compliments all around, everyone being unusually cordial. Rose and Aunt Ida had carried on a conversation all their own and disappeared with Ozzie as soon as dinner was over. At Matt's prompting, Tom had driven Mr. Schmidt around Branbury for half an hour, to the old man's uttermost pleasure.

As Evie had helped Murphy put away the folding chairs, she asked, "Is Matt always this way at mealtime—always making trouble?"

And Murphy had turned, his face working up to an answer, and said, "N . . . ot so much. He's not any t . . . rouble." And then he had smiled widely, adding, "Pa Hutchins says he's like a b . . . rother to me."

So he was like a brother to Murphy and a son to Dad, and meanwhile he said things at the table that Evie would never have been allowed to say herself.

It was this that infuriated her. Matt came bringing with him all the impertinent questions that she had hidden so carefully all these years, even from herself. Matt waded right in where angels feared to tread, and Father treated him like a little lost lamb.

"I won't have anyone at my table looking down on someone . . ." he had said, and his voice was clear and strong, just as it was from the pulpit.

At a time when Evie herself felt buffeted by doubts and uncertainties, when she had hoped that the occasion would be a reconciliation not only between Rose and Donna Jean but between the warring parts of herself, Matt had dragged those doubts to the table and passed them around, one by one.

Someone was coming down the path. Evie sensed it by the way the sheep moved to one side. And it was Matt himself who came over and stood beside her. She turned away, not trusting herself to speak.

"You mad or something?"

She clamped her teeth together. "Or something," she hissed, and continued to stare at the far slope and the jungle of honeysuckle. Frank Kettle glanced over at them and went on packing dirt around a marker he had just raised.

Matt lowered himself down on the other end of the flat gravestone where Evie sat. "I teed you off yesterday, didn't I?"

"Good Lord, Matt, you teed everybody off." She was half shouting, almost on the verge of tears. "You just open your mouth and say whatever rolls off the end of your tongue. You don't think how it's going to sound or who's present or what the occasion. You just say the first stupid thing that comes to mind."

"I wasn't trying to be smart. I really meant it. It's just something I was wondering about."

"You've been living at my place for two months! How come you just happened to wonder about it at a dinner for Donna Jean and Tom? How come you had to bring it up the first time I came home for a visit? I wonder about things too, but I know enough to keep my mouth shut."

He looked at her quizzically. "What do *you* talk about at the table? 'Pass the butter?' 'Need more salt'?" His eyes snapped too. "I hardly even had a dad to talk to. You do, but all you talk about are safe things that never get anybody stirred up."

"I can talk about anything I like with my father."

"Yeah?"

"But I certainly don't do it in front of Aunt Ida, for one."

"Why? She got a heart condition or something? It's your home. If you can't stay what you feel, you better kick the tenants out."

"Well, you'll be the first to go." Evie's eyes blazed. "There's such a thing as getting along with people, Matt Jewel. There's such a thing as keeping the conversation pleasant and trying not to hurt anybody, of knowing what's appropriate and what's not."

"What am I supposed to do? Put my mind in the deep freeze? Listen, Evie, you know what struck me the first time I ate at your place? All the people!

I mean that as a compliment. As long as I could remember, practically—since Dad left, anyway—it was just Mom and me at the table. Every time we said anything, the other knew what it was going to be. No surprises. And suddenly, at your place, there were people all around. I thought it would be a real experience, you know? Six or seven people, with company thrown in on Sunday—six or seven ideas all going at once."

He shook his head. "Well, there's hardly ever more than one idea going around the table, and it's served up as the main course by your mother or aunt or Rose. Anybody else tries an idea that's a little different, everybody takes a nibble and makes a face."

"Just where do you get off, Matt?" Evie swung her legs over the edge and straightened up, too angry now to cry. "My father hired you to help around outside, not to overhaul the family." She saw Frank Kettle pick up his tools and go trudging off to the toolshed. "I don't *want* to know what you think, I don't *want* to know what you don't believe, I don't want you messing around with my head or my life!"

His face softened. "Evie, you're supposed to be the deep thinker. You're the one who's always writing down feelings. You're the one who's interested in what the Indians said, what the Chinese said, old Russian proverbs—"

She leaped off the tombstone, the rage finding its target.

"You've been reading my journal!"

He stared.

"You've been snooping around in my things!"

"Hey, wait a minute! I was only moving the blankets out of that chest. I just read a couple pages. I really *liked* it, Evie."

"Well, you can just go back to Waldorf, for all I care." Her voice was high and tight. "I'm sick of you and everything about you. Every time you open your mouth, it's wrong, wrong, wrong. Just don't come to the Rawleys any more to see me. As far as you're concerned, I'm not there."

She wheeled around and went stiffly up the path to the back slope, her heart pounding fiercely, fists clenched, nails digging into her palms. Angry tears stung her eyes. It was a relief to have it out, to finally tell him off. She should have done it long ago. Lord, how she hated Matt Jewel!

Frank Kettle stood in the door of the toolshed, watching her come. As she passed, he said, "It's no good letting the sun set on a quarrel, Evie. Lots of folks under the ground and lots of folks on top would have give anything for a second chance."

"Tell it to Matt Jewel," she said, and went on back to Donna Jean's.

It was Thursday the tenth when it happened. For days afterwards, Evie had stared at the calendar, at that single square of white, with nothing more innocuous than "call store about paint" scribbled in pencil.

Twelve fifteen: Chris stopped by with a quart of milk and a submarine sandwich. Evie sat on the swing while he ate, holding Josh on her lap, his bare feet in her hands. She softly patted the soles together as they rocked, making him grunt with pleasure. He even fussed when Donna Jean came for him, so content he was with Evie.

"I'm going to buy another tom-tom," Chris told her. "A twelve-inch. I've just about saved enough from Hollander's to buy it."

They walked back to the road, enjoying the coolness of the lane which, even at noon, was partially shaded.

"You're going to have so many drums you won't be able to get them in the car," Evie kidded. "Next summer you'll stay in Silver Spring because you won't be able to move them."

He laughed and put an arm around her. "Oh, I'll probably come. Dad will be here for a few more years yet."

The "probably" and the "yet" depressed her. Was she only a summertime girl friend in a one-horse town, where the hottest thing going on Saturday night was the highway grocery?

He sensed her quiet and jiggled her shoulder. "Hey—you're off in space somewhere. Still worried about Matt? Because of what you said to him?"

"No, I'm not worried about Matt."

"Good. I thought maybe the four of us could do something this weekend."

"Make it the three of you, then. If Matt's along, I'm not interested."

"You really *do* hold a grudge, don't you?" They had reached the end of the lane, and he stood with his hands on her waist, facing her. "It bothers him that you're mad. He told me."

"So let it."

He held her out away from him, imitating her pout, then laughed and kissed her, and she went back to the Rawleys' feeling vaguely out of sorts.

One ten: Donna Jean had just given Josh his bath. While he was being diapered, Evie picked up the rubber kitten she had bought him, holding it above his face and squeezing it to make a loud squeak. Joshua blinked and lay very still, staring, his blue eyes wide. Evie squeaked it again, and this time brought it closer and closer to his bare tummy, till it squeaked against his skin.

And then he laughed, a soft small chuckle.

"He laughed!" Donna Jean said. "Evie, he did it for you! His very first laugh."

Delighted, Evie tried it again. It was a strange sound, like a laugh that needed practice, but a chuckle nevertheless.

"Oh, Josh," Donna Jean said, picking him up and hugging him. "Your daddy is going to be so pleased!

He's really a little person now, isn't he, Evie? He has a laugh all his own."

Evie kissed one of the chubby pink feet, smelling of talcum, the toes curled under. *Her* baby, definitely.

"Have a good nap, Josh," she said, and emptied the pan of water while Donna Jean took him upstairs.

The afternoon was spent at hard labor, as Donna Jean called it, scraping the paint off some old doors that they had bought for countertops.

Four fifty-two. Tom was home.

"Hey, wait a minute," he said, as Donna Jean tried to lift one of the doors off the sawhorses. "I'll do that." He put down his briefcase and propped the heavy door against a wall. He found a few rough places she had missed and began sanding them down. "Where's Matt lately, Evie? Haven't seen him all week."

"I don't miss him."

"No?" Tom cocked his head. "Still mad at him about last Sunday?"

"He has this ingenious way of stirring up trouble. He thrives on it. It makes his hair grow."

"Didn't stir up anything that wasn't in the pot already," Donna Jean told her.

"The way he attacked my father's sermon. . . ."

Tom stopped sanding. "That wasn't an attack, girl, it was a question. There's a difference." He brushed the sawdust off his trousers. "You know, you can be loyal to your father and still disagree with him. Just because you don't see eye-to-eye with him doesn't mean you've stopped loving him. Maybe Matt's questions stirred up something in yourself. Ever think of that?"

Evie went on sanding and made no reply.

Five twenty-one: "We need a break," Donna Jean said. "I'm going to wake Josh up, or he'll be all off schedule. Evie, do we have any lemonade left from lunch? Let's go out on the porch awhile."

If only time had stopped there. The details of what happened next were imprisoned forever in Evie's head: the feel of the cold pitcher in her hands as she lifted it from the refrigerator, the calendar there above the sink, the sound of Donna Jean's footsteps on the stairs and Tom opening his briefcase on the dining room table. . . .

And then, the moment Evie would remember all her life—the strange patter of running feet on the floor above, the thud on the stairs. . . .

"Tom!"

Donna Jean's voice sounded choked, raspy, dry, as though words were caught in her throat. Evie set the pitcher on the table and came out of the kitchen to find her cousin halfway down the stairs, leaning against the wall, doubled over, hands on her abdomen, as though she had been kicked. Her face was as white as cream.

"Donna Jean?" Tom came in from the next room.

And suddenly Donna Jean threw back her head, her throat thick, the muscles straining, and her lips opened wide without a sound, as though even a scream could not get through.

Tom grabbed her. "Donna Jean!"

The scream came: "Josh!"

Tom lunged upstairs while Evie stood paralyzed in the doorway. For a moment there was no noise at all, not a sound from anyone. Donna Jean remained fixed on the stairs, her head back, mouth open, eyes tightly shut; she did not even appear to be breathing. And then the cry came from Tom:

"My god! Oh, my god!"

Evie ran past Donna Jean to the hallway above.

Tom was standing in the doorway of his bedroom holding the baby. There was something terribly wrong. Josh did not move. His tiny hands were extended upwards, just a little, like those of a china doll. Evie came closer, a heaviness settling on her chest.

Tom shook his head unbelievingly. "He's dead, Evie!" he whispered. "My baby's dead."

Once, when Evie was at the ocean, a wave had taken her off guard. She had been knocked off her feet and tumbled over and over, a rushing roar in her ears, the breath sucked from her, until she was deposited once more on the sand.

It seemed to have happened again now, some force pulling her under. She told herself this could not be; Josh had not even been sick. She herself had made him laugh. She herself had felt the warmth of that little foot, had smelled the fragrance of talcumed skin.

She made her way downstairs, her legs rubbery, past Donna Jean who was gasping and gulping, and grabbed the phone in the kitchen. She told the doctor's nurse that there was an emergency at the Rawleys', and then leaned against the refrigerator with her hands over her ears, eyes tightly closed, drowning out the sobs from the stairway. *No!* she screamed silently inside her head. *Not Josh! Not her soul child!*

She remembered praying for it to be a mistake and—were it not a mistake—for a miracle. Surely the God who had saved the Israelites from the Red Sea and the men in the fiery furnace could look gently down from heaven now on behalf of Joshua John.

She was aware of the doctor's presence in the hallway, of an ambulance driver, of footsteps upstairs and people coming and going, of questions asked, questions answered, and the constant accompaniment of weeping. Another car in the clearing, another man, more footsteps, questions, papers. . . . It did not seem possible, but when she looked at the clock again, it was after seven.

She was sitting at the kitchen table, her head buried in her arms, when the doctor came in and sat down by her.

Evie looked up. "Is he really dead?"

"Yes."

"Why?" The tears she had held back came rushing now, along with the anger. "*Why?*"

The doctor put one big hand on hers. "I don't know. A crib death. No one is really sure how it happens."

"He wasn't even sick!" She would argue him out of it. She *had* to.

"Most of the babies aren't. Perhaps it's an allergic reaction, but it's one of the saddest things we see. They go to bed seemingly happy and healthy, and then they die. Joshua has been dead for several hours."

Evie put her head down on the table again, crying hard. "If only I had gone up to check."

"Listen." His voice was firm. "Whenever there's a crib death, that's the first thing the parents think of: if only they had done this or that. In the next few weeks, Tom and Donna Jean will ask themselves a thousand questions for which there are no answers. Did they feed him something they shouldn't have? Overlook a cold? And each time, no matter what it is, you will have to remind them that it just happened, and there was probably nothing they could have done to prevent it."

She nodded, hands over her face.

"I asked Donna Jean whom I should notify, and she said no one," the doctor told her. "They say they want to be alone, but the coroner is making his report, and people are going to hear. You'll have to be their link to the community, Evie. And that may be the most difficult thing you've ever done."

She watched from the window as the small bundle was carried from the house to the waiting ambulance. Neither Tom nor Donna Jean accompanied it. Long after the coroner had left, and finally the doctor, Donna Jean remained on the stairs, her face contorted with grief, the wall next to her cheek damp where her tears had soaked into the plaster.

Evie sat helplessly a few steps below her, sickened by her own pain. "I'm here, Donna Jean," she wept softly. "If there's anything you want me to do. . . ."

There was no reply. Tom had gone out into the back yard and wandered dazedly among the trees, plodding through the garden, stepping on bean plants, his arms dangling strangely at his sides.

Evie walked back and forth between the stairway and the kitchen window. Why couldn't they share it, the two of them? Why, after all these years of closeness were they so separate now in their grief? Why, in this greatest test of love, did they seem to abandon each other?

Then the back screen opened and Tom came at last. He was on the stairs beside Donna Jean and had her in his arms. Evie went out on the porch and sat in the swing, head tipped back, salty tears running down her throat, a thousand thoughts spinning through her mind.

Her parents were the first to arrive, as she had known they would be. Whenever a resident of Branbury went to the hospital in LaPlata, someone called the Hutchinses. Whenever there was a death or an accident, whenever a home burned down, someone always thought to call Evie's father. She got up from the swing and went out to the car to meet them. Engulfed in her father's arms, she let herself cry again.

Mrs. Hutchins was weeping too. "To think that last Sunday I held him in my arms," she said.

They walked together to the porch. "I told the Lord this evening that I didn't understand," Evie's father said. "I told Him that if we ever needed His strength, it was now."

"I'm not sure they'll want to see anybody," Evie said. But she led them through the hallway, and Tom got up off the stairs to meet them. He and Evie's father embraced and held each other a minute, but Donna Jean turned away and leaned her face once more against the wall.

Other cars were arriving, and eventually Donna Jean was persuaded to sit at the kitchen table. Evie met the callers at the door and urged them to stay only a few minutes.

As Mrs. Hutchins left, she put an arm around

her daughter and said, "Tell her, dear, for me, that the Lord never gives us more than we can bear. If He gave her this burden, He'll give her the strength to bear it. That she can believe."

Evie did not answer.

Long after the Hutchinses left, friends kept coming. Sue Shields drove up with her parents, but sat in the car and cried while they went inside. Loaves of bread wrapped in tinfoil appeared on the kitchen counter—a pie, a cake. A barbequed chicken, still warm from the oven, was placed on top the stove.

"She'll not feel like cooking for a while," one woman explained as she slipped a Jello salad in the refrigerator.

No, Evie thought. *Or eating, ever again.*

Around nine, Tom and Donna Jean went upstairs, and Evie told those who arrived later that the Rawleys had gone to bed. But she herself could not sleep. She sat on the swing, oblivious to the mosquitoes, too numb to feel weary.

And then there were footsteps in the hallway and Tom and Donna Jean came out on the porch.

"We're going to get Josh," they told her, and got in the car.

Thirteen

A COOL WIND SWEPT over the porch. Evie sat huddled on the steps next to a post. The feathery network of dark branches against the night sky seemed like a web, trapping her in a nightmare she could not believe. As late visitors arrived, she told them that the Rawleys were gone, and they left their condolences with her.

Over by the trees, a lone figure stood with shoulders hunched, hands in his pockets, awkward.

Not him. As much as she longed for someone to talk to, she did not long for Matt. She was overpowered by unhappiness and could not bear any more.

He came over.

"I heard," was all he said. And finally, when she did not respond, "Lord, Evie, I'm so sorry for them."

She stared stonily ahead.

"Is there anything I can do?" he asked finally.

"Yes," she told him. "Go home."

He did not move, but stood looking down at her, and finally she put her head in her lap, weary, closing her eyes, hoping that when she opened them again, he would be gone. He was.

About midnight, after she had crept inside and stood watching from the window, the brush along the lane grew brighter as the headlights of a car approached, and then the Dodge pulled up and stopped. Donna Jean walked slowly to the house, carrying Joshua.

"The coroner said we could keep him here till morning," Tom said. "We didn't really have a chance to say goodbye."

Upstairs, the creak of the rocking chair in the Rawleys' bedroom ticked off the hours as the night passed. Evie sat on the floor in the hallway, where she had kept her vigil at the baby's birth. The white hospital sheet that had covered him when he left had been replaced with his own blanket of green and yellow, his name embroidered in one corner. Donna Jean sang softly to the baby who could not hear her. From time to time, Tom took Joshua from her and walked slowly about the room, talking to the son he had no longer.

Once he went out into the backyard where he had paced alone that evening. As Evie watched from her darkened window, her eyelids burning, she saw him take the baby around and introduce him to the big oak there in one corner, to the small garden plot, the bird feeder, the shed, the tree stump . . . all the things he must have planned to show Josh later.

Just before dawn, when Evie had resumed her watch in the hallway, Tom knelt down beside her.

"Would you like to say goodbye?" he whispered.

She nodded and held out her arms, and then she was holding the baby—her special baby—for the last time.

No warmth penetrated the blanket. The small body was stiff, unbending. Already there was a slight smell of decay about it, and yet it was Joshua still. Evie bent over gently and kissed his fine red hair. She tried to remember what her last words to him had been: *Have a good nap.*

They rode back to the hospital together. It was too early for Friday traffic, and the road, the hills, seemed to belong to them alone. Near a misty glen, Donna Jean suddenly asked Tom to pull over.

She got out, Tom behind her, and walked a few yards into a meadow. Evie stood beside the car, wondering—shivering in the cool morning air. Standing calf-deep in clover and milkweed, the trees shadowy clumps of gray, Donna Jean held the quilted bundle to her breast and, looking up at the morning star, said firmly, "Joshua John, in the name of Christ, please come back to us."

Evie stared uncomprehendingly. She looked at Tom for some sign of reason and was even more surprised when he dropped to his knees and added, "Dear God, we ask that our child be given back to us, if only for a day, an hour. . . ." He waited, eyes tightly closed.

Evie leaned against the car, her eyes on the sky. But there was no voice from the clouds, no rending of the heavens, and the morning star, white overhead, did not even flicker. Had they then, for a moment, believed? And did they disbelieve now?

They did not speak again on their way to the hospital. Evie waited in the car while the Rawleys went inside. When they came out at last, even the green and yellow blanket had been left behind.

Heading home, Donna Jean murmured to no one in particular, "It was something we had to do. We would never have forgiven ourselves if we hadn't tried."

And then she began to sob, Tom with her, and Evie let her own tears come again as well. They cried openly, and the grief came gushing up.

"Do you know how I feel?" Donna Jean said at last as they turned in the lane. "Homesick. A crushing feeling of loneliness. Like I'm far away and want to come back, but it will never be home again without Joshua."

The Rawleys went to bed, but Evie could not. Someone might call, come by. It was almost morning. She felt dizzy from lack of food and sleep. The yellow cat meowed loudly at the back door, and Evie placed some milk and ham on the stoop for him.

Slowly the shadowy objects about the yard became more distinct as the sky brightened. She sat at the kitchen table, her head buried in her arms. Her mind floated off into fragments of dreams, returned, then drifted away again.

Joshua John was alive in her dreams—talking and walking; in fact, *I'm here*, he announced to the mourners who sat about the Rawley kitchen staring at him, and Evie followed him elatedly as he toddled about, wondering why no one shared her joy.

Only the ache in her shoulders woke her. She opened her eyes, conscious of the stiffness in her neck. As she raised her head, she saw her father sitting across from her.

"Dad?"

"I didn't want to wake you, honey." He was slouched as though he had been sitting a long time. Evie pressed her fingers against her eyes. "We've been up all night. They went to get Josh."

"I know. The hospital called. They thought perhaps someone should be with them, but I knew that you would see them through."

She looked at her father and saw absolute trust looking back. Panic flitted about in her stomach.

"I thought you'd need a good sleep, so I'm going to take over," he told her. "Go to bed. I'll handle the calls and the visitors."

She got up and started toward the stairs, then turned. "Dad . . . this morning . . . when they were taking Joshua back, they stopped by the side of the road and prayed. They asked God to give him back." She waited, trying to read her father's eyes. "Would there have been a miracle, do you think, if Tom and Donna Jean really believed?"

Mr. Hutchins shook his head. "I think that whatever was going to happen happened. God didn't give Joshua back because He never took him away. I can't believe He would go around taking little eight-week-old babies just because the parents had doubts."

She had wanted to say more, but felt drained of all feeling. In her weariness, all she could manage was, "I have doubts, too."

His eyes looked back at her like mirrors reflected in mirrors, going deeper and deeper inside himself, till Evie felt lost.

"We'll talk later, honey," he said at last. "Try to sleep now if you can."

She lay on her bed, but her mind was alive with images and a steady parade of faces passed by— faces she had never seen, yet finely detailed, as though she were really meeting them on the street. Every so often the faces were interrupted by that of her father's, by eyes that revealed themselves, layer after layer. He would look after things while she slept. She could count on it. And at last, sleep took over.

It was eleven-thirty when she woke. Friday. How was it possible that only a day had passed since Joshua's death, when it seemed that they had been mourning him for a week? Her body did not want to move, to involve itself in all that was to come.

Slowly grief settled over her again, as though the ceiling were descending and sadness crushing her chest. This was Joshua's yellow room no longer. What would they do with the toy cupboard, so lovingly constructed, the crib, the clothes? How could Donna Jean ever bear to touch something that was once his?

She thought of Tom and Donna Jean during the pregnancy—the laughter, the jokes, the fondness, the backrubs. . . . Now there was pain and shock and anger and sadness, and it seemed to Evie that it might have been better had they never married at all. Each time you attached yourself to someone, each time you really cared, you took on the possibility of grief as well. The more people you had to love, the more there were to worry about.

She went into the bath to shower and noticed that the door to the Rawleys' room was open. The bed was unmade, but empty, the house strangely quiet. When she went downstairs later, she found not her father but Aunt Ida, who was going over the floors with a dust mop.

"Don't see how she expects to keep things clean with all this sawdust about," Aunt Ida said.

Evie stared at her, dumbfounded, then went into

the kitchen without answering and poured some cereal. But her aunt came after her and began wiping the top of the stove.

"Where is everyone?" Evie asked finally. Her lips barely moved.

"Out to see about a cemetery lot. Want to dig the grave themselves, that's what they told your father. It's none of my concern, of course, but folks are going to be coming by all day to pay their respects, and you'd think the Rawleys would want to be here."

She thrust the frying pan in the sink and attacked it with the scraper. Evie ate silently, knowing that when Tom and Donna Jean came back and the tears began again, she would probably eat nothing more the rest of the day. And then she heard her aunt saying, "They tell me Tom and Donna Jean went to the morgue last night and talked the coroner into letting them take the baby home. Now if that isn't the most heathen thing I ever heard of, Evie! Why, I could hardly believe my ears."

The food caught in Evie's throat, and she felt she would choke if she swallowed. Then suddenly the gray-haired woman plunked down in a chair and cried.

"Oh, my, the poor little tyke! I never had a child of my own, Evie, and wouldn't know what it was to lose one. But oh, how it must hurt! How it must hurt!"

Evie stood on the front steps, wondering whether or not she should go to the cemetery and help. She decided it was something personal that Tom and Donna Jean would prefer to do alone.

Chris appeared in the lane, and she walked slowly out to meet him.

"I'm on my lunch break, so I can't stay long," he told her. "Somebody came by Hollander's and told us about Josh. I didn't figure you'd want me to come by last night. I just didn't know what to do."

"Nobody does."

"How did it happen?"

"We're not sure. The coroner said it was probably an unusual flash reaction to a pneumonia germ. But it doesn't really make any difference now."

"Do you feel like walking?"

"A little, maybe."

They moved down the lane. Evie broke off a laurel leaf and idly pinched it to pieces in her fingers, dropping a section here, another there.

"It must have been awful for you," Chris said at last.

"And for them."

"I guess so." He waited a minute. "Is there anything I can do? Send flowers or something?"

"Flowers won't help. There's just nothing, really. But I'll tell them you offered."

"Yeah. I'll only be around another week. I mean, if there *is* anything I can do. Mom wants me to come home early so we can go to the ocean before I register at the college."

It seemed strange to Evie that there was any

summer left, as though, when Joshua died, he had taken it with him. Stranger still that Chris could be talking about the ocean and college at a time like this. Then the reality of what he had told her sunk in. Another week and he would be gone.

"I'd really like to stay longer," he continued. "I need the money, and . . . well, we won't have too much time together with the funeral and all."

There seemed to be something wrong with the translation as it was decoded in Evie's head.

"Yes, the funeral is so horribly inconvenient, isn't it?"

He glanced at her. "I didn't mean it like that at all."

"It doesn't matter."

"Why?"

"Nothing matters. People plan for something and then it never works out. Look how much Josh meant to them." Her chin trembled. "He was the biggest thing in their lives, and then—just like that—he's gone."

"But if you never reach out for anything. . . ."

"Then you won't be disappointed," she finished bitterly. "Joshua's gone, you're leaving, everything's changed."

He stopped, facing her, and then put his hands on her shoulders. "I'm coming back next summer."

"Sure. If your father's not transferred or your

mother doesn't make other plans or you don't get a job in Silver Spring or meet somebody else. . . ."

She wondered why he didn't just push her away, all her bitterness and spite and anger, but instead he gently pulled her to him, and then her head was on his chest and she was crying.

"It could happen to you too, Evie. You could get a job somewhere or a chance to travel or you might meet somebody else. . . ."

She knew, she knew. Not only were there no guarantees about the other people in her life, she couldn't even be sure of herself.

When Tom and Donna Jean came back about four, they simply sat down on the porch with the mud of Joshua's burial place on their feet and greeted the guests that came and went. Mrs. Hutchins had replaced Aunt Ida in the kitchen.

It was almost six when Evie slipped away. The sun was low over the dogwoods and the rays came through at a peculiar angle, warming only one side of her face. She reached the tangle of honeysuckle and made her way down the slope.

Beyond the stream, Tom had told her. *Where the wild strawberries grow.* She followed the winding path and there, beneath an aging oak, was the grave for Joshua.

She had to see it, feel it, to know what it was like where Josh was going—to share this with him.

Dropping down on her knees she looked into the hole. The sides were roughly hewn, not nearly as smooth as Frank Kettle would have made them, showing jagged marks from the shovel's tip. The hole was not as wide or as long or even as deep as an ordinary grave, but it seemed just right for Joshua. No, not right at all.

She turned and plucked the long grass growing among the tombstones that the sheep hadn't reached. Gently she gathered handful after handful and dropped it down into Joshua's grave. Clover, too. The handfuls became armfuls until at last there was a soft blanket of green for the baby.

Gently, so as not to disturb the edges, Evie slipped over the side and crouched down, touching the grass with her hands, patting it in place. Then she lay on her back, her knees bent, and looked up at the purple sky.

This was where it ended, then—the birth pains, the delivery, the nursing, the worry. This was what it all came to—soft coos and milky breath exchanged for the damp smell of grass and roots.

I don't want this baby, Donna had wailed at the height of her pain, and somehow the gods—God?—had heard. Evie put her hands over her face and wept.

"Evie?"

She gulped, cutting off a sob, and listened. Someone had followed her there, seen her climb in, heard her weep. And then Frank Kettle was reaching down his leathery hand and helping her up.

She sat on the ground across from him and finished her cry. She didn't really want him here, didn't want him to touch her. Irrational, but there it was.

"I got to even it up a little before dark," he told her. "Didn't want to do it with them around, but the corners aren't true, and the coffin might not fit."

She nodded, knowing he meant no harm.

"I just wanted to know what it was like," she said by way of explanation, getting up.

He nodded. "Everybody's curious, but we'll all find out soon enough, I reckon."

The funeral took place on Saturday morning at sunrise. Donna Jean and Tom had expressed their wishes to a few close friends, and the message was passed along. There were to be no cars winding down into the cemetery, no sermon, no formal bouquets. Everything was to be kept natural and childlike, but all were welcome.

There was no sunshine as Evie had hoped, but fog. Shadowy figures left their parked cars on the highway above and walked down the long road to the oak tree beyond the stream, muted flashes of color in the swirling mist. The tops of trees seemed to evaporate into nothingness as the clouds rolled in, and there was a certain crispness to the air that signaled autumn.

Evie and Tom and Donna Jean walked together. Earlier that morning they had driven to the hospital for the last time and brought Joshua home in his green and yellow blanket. Murphy, they had been told, had stayed up all night making a small coffin of pine—gentle, loving Murphy, whose hands could do wonders, it seemed, beyond the reach of his mind.

Now, as they approached the small circle of friends and neighbors around the grave, they saw the pine box, its lid open. For a moment Donna Jean hesitated. Then, at Tom's quiet bidding, she stepped bravely forward, smiling just a little at the friends who had gathered. Murphy stood behind the casket, mouth agape, eyes fixed. Rose, in dark glasses, and Aunt Ida in her black hat, stood in a row beside Mr. and Mrs. Hutchins, which meant that neighbors had volunteered to stay at home with Mr. Schmidt and Sister Ozzie.

Evie saw Chris and Sue and Matt standing together on the other side of the grave. She exchanged glances with Chris, and he gave her a gentle nod. She avoided Matt's eyes entirely.

When all were assembled, a friend of Tom's lifted his guitar and played "Down in the Valley," not singing the words, just humming the melody through half-open lips, like a lullaby. He followed it with "Amazing Grace," and some of the church people joined in.

Evie found that she could not sing. Tears seeped

perpetually from her eyes. She had promised herself that she would be strong, someone the Rawleys could depend on. Instead, she felt weak and useless, dabbing at her eyes with Kleenex, her lips trembling. Where was God's power now, the power her father had spoken of so convincingly? Certainly not here.

When the music was over, the guitarist picked up a basket of wild flowers. He said a few words about how the flowers had been picked just that morning, barely an hour before, but were wilting already, a reminder of how short our lives really were. He said that he would pass the basket around, and each person could take one in memory of Joshua John and share a few words if he liked.

The basket moved slowly in the other direction, away from Evie. Some people took a flower and passed the basket on. But now and then the basket stopped temporarily, and someone said that the spirit of Josh was eternal, or that it wasn't the end of hope. Mrs. Hutchins said she was convinced that someday Donna Jean and Tom would see their child again, but to Evie, the thought seemed out of place. This was a time for accepting death, for grappling with it—respecting it, even. She glanced at Donna Jean, but the pale freckled face rested on Tom's shoulder, eyes closed, face serene—grateful, it seemed, for every word that was spoken, as though intended as a gift for her.

When his turn came, Evie's father said that the joy that Joshua had already brought his parents was something that could never be taken away, it was theirs to keep, and Evie was dismayed to find herself weeping again.

The basket passed silently from Sue to Matt to Chris, and when Evie glanced over again, she saw Matt looking at her soberly, intently. She looked away. The basket was coming around the far side of the circle now, and soon it would be her turn.

Her brain seemed a block of ice, frozen and numb. She could not organize her thoughts coherently, could not put into words what she was feeling. After all these months with Joshua—closer to him than anyone outside his parents—she felt too self-conscious and tearful to say anything at all. The moment would pass her by. Her cheeks burned, her throat felt constricted. Slowly the basket came toward her, paused for a moment as a man said a prayer, and then it was in her hands.

Blindly her fingers groped for one of the flowers, and she gulped, clutching the basket to her, not wanting to let it go. But she could think of nothing. Nothing.

And then, from across the circle, she heard someone say, "If it's all right with Evie, I'd like to say something for her, something that was once said by a Blackfoot Indian chief."

Evie lifted her eyes and blinked through her wet

lashes. Matt was standing as he always did, shoulders hunched, hands in his pockets. But his soft voice carried distinctly around the circle:

" 'What is life?
It is the breath of a buffalo in wintertime.
It is the little shadow
    Which runs across the grass
    And loses itself in the sunset.' "

Matt. She could not see him now, for the tears came too fast. She heard Donna Jean murmur appreciatively and felt the touch of her hand as she took the basket. The verse had been perfect for Joshua.

How could Matt have known? How was he able, through all her turmoil and sadness and anger, to pick up her own sensitivities and choose the very lines that had been her favorite? Guilt from one direction collided with remorse from the other. Her thoughts tumbled about in confusion. Somehow she would catch Matt's eye and thank him. But when the tears stopped and she looked across the circle, she saw him standing with head down, thoughtful.

The guitar player began once more, a young woman sang, and then it was time to bury Joshua.

Tom handed the quilted bundle to his wife, and she slowly pulled back a corner, exposing Joshua's perfectly shaped head for the last time. But the face looked gray. Gently, gently, without tears, as though buoyed by some inner peace, Donna Jean kissed her baby. And then they were both kneeling together and placing the blanketed baby in the coffin. Evie steadied herself as she felt her body sway.

The lid had been made to slide in place, so there would be no pounding. Tom leaned over and put his hand on the baby's head. *Goodbye, Josh*, he mouthed, and the lid slid shut. He climbed down in the hole, picked up the coffin in his arms, and bent over, out of sight, placing his son on the bed of grass and clover.

Tom climbed out of the grave. From the mound of fresh earth, he grabbed one of two shovels. Donna took the other. They plunged them into the dirt, but it was heavy and damp, and each seemed to have trouble lifting. The first clump of earth fell, a hollow sound on the lid of the casket. Evie watched them moving in unison, throwing themselves into the task. It was something they had said they wanted to do by themselves, but it was awkward—the others standing helplessly by.

Then Evie's father stepped forward and put his hand on Tom's shoulder. "Let me have that shovel for a while," he said. "That's my child in there, too."

Tom looked puzzled. But he handed it over, and after a few turns, the guitar player took it, then Murphy. One of Donna Jean's friends took the shovel from her and then, as Evie stared, it was Rose who stepped up and asked to help.

Donna Jean stood back, grateful. "You don't know how much this means to us," she kept saying. "We wanted to do it ourselves, but. . . ."

"He belonged to all of us, Donna Jean," Mr. Hutchins said.

The shovels passed on.

They had all gone back to the Rawleys' house but Evie. She could not leave the little mound of earth beneath the oak tree, circled with stones, strewn with flowers from the basket. She knew she would not be missed.

She could not escape the irrational feeling that somehow, if she could only hold Josh in her arms once more, her breath, her warmth, might bring him back. Evie had never so much as left him alone on the porch in his stroller. How could she possibly go away and leave him here? Her little soul child, the shadow lost in the sunset. . . .

And then she realized that someone else had stayed behind. Her father sat on a tombstone a few yards off, waiting for her.

She put her grief into words: "It's like they've all walked out on him. Even God." She was all choked up, her nose clogged.

"Not God, honey."

"Where is He, then?" Defiant. Angry.

"He's here."

She rose up on her knees beside the grave. "Where? Down there with Josh?" she asked harshly.

"Everywhere. With Josh, with you, with Donna Jean and Tom. . . ."

"Then why did He let it happen?"

"I don't know, Evie. I don't understand His plan. I don't believe that he intended for Joshua to die, but now that it's happened, I think He will use it in some way for the best, to somehow glorify His creation."

Evie stood up and her throat felt tight. "Why couldn't He let Josh grow up into a fine young man? Why wouldn't *that* glorify His creation?"

"We must trust Him, Evie. I believe with all my heart that when the final hour comes, we will see God's purpose—so vast and glorious that all the suffering we have endured will have a place."

"Dad, those are just words! It wasn't God's will that Josh should die, you said, just some vast and glorious plan." Her eyes blazed and she found herself half-shouting: "You go around contradicting yourself! You say things like 'glorify His creation' without any meaning behind them, and when a person tries to understand them, piece by piece, they fall apart. They all add up to the same thing: if we wait long enough, till we're dead or the world ends or something, then we'll understand."

She was crying. "Well, that's too late. If God expects me to wait till Judgment Day to understand Him, He can wait till Judgment Day for me to worship Him."

Her father's face was drawn: "That's where faith comes in, Evie."

"*Words*, Dad! Words! I want to know in simple everyday language why Joshua had to die and why God didn't save him and why, now that he's gone, I should believe in anything at all."

Her father stood up slowly, as though not quite trusting his legs, and every line on his face seemed to be cut deeper.

"Turn on me, Evie, if you want, but don't go turning your back on God. I know I don't have the education that some preachers do, and I wish I had the power to move mountains, but don't let anything I say come between you and the Lord."

"You won't come between me and anybody, Dad, because there's no one there."

"Evie!"

She fled from him then, at the first sign of his arms stretching out toward her, and rushed back up the path. She had to do it; someone had to do it for Joshua. Someone had to protest his death. She couldn't let him lie there beneath the ground, never to laugh his little laugh again, without someone rebuking whatever it was that had put him there.

For hours she lay on her bed upstairs as people

moved in and out of the rooms below. She had hurt her father, she knew. Even worse, she had meant to do it. But had she said what she did for Josh or for herself?

One thing was certain: the words separated her somehow from the girl she had once been. She had announced a new direction, a private search, and they would both have to reckon with that.

Fourteen

CHRIS LEFT BRANBURY a week later. His father drove him over to say goodbye, the drums taking up the entire space in the back of the Chevy. Mr. Lundgren sat in the car and read a newspaper while Chris came to the door and kissed Evie for the last time.

"I'm not much on writing," he said, "but I'll call you now and then. Hollander said he'll hire me next summer if I'm here by June first. And I'll probably be down over Christmas to see Dad."

"Let me know when you get your new tom-tom," she said.

"Yeah, I will." He smiled. "Maybe I'll play something for you over the phone."

She watched the car pull out. The drums were the last to disappear. She turned and went back through the house.

Donna Jean was sitting on the back stoop. She was barefoot and still wearing the light robe she had put on for breakfast. Her hair was uncombed, and she leaned silently against the doorframe, staring out over the unwatered, unweeded garden.

"I'll get to those beans this afternoon," Evie told her, sitting down.

There was no reply. The yellow cat came slouching and stretching up the path, rubbed its back against the edge of the stoop, then put one paw in Donna Jean's lap.

"Get *out* of here!" Donna Jean flung her arm out and pushed the cat away, then stood up and went inside.

Evie sat morosely by the back door. It was as though Joshua had taken everything with him—their plans, their joy, their warmth, their sharing. The Rawleys seemed a family no longer, just two aching people nursing a raw wound that a look, a word, a thing remembered could expose once again.

They seemed to inhabit different worlds, Evie thought—Tom and Donna Jean. Summer school was over, but Tom spent his mornings preparing his lessons for fall. In the afternoons he would walk relentlessly over the fields, covering miles in a single day. When he came home he would ask, "Where's Donna Jean?" and the answer was always the same: *lying down*, or sometimes, *out on the back stoop*.

He would go to her, rub her shoulders, attempt

conversation. But she seldom responded at all. Finally he would give up and sit on the porch alone.

Evie mentioned one night at dinner that perhaps it was time for her to leave. "I thought you might like to have some time to yourselves without me always around," she told them.

Donna Jean looked up from her plate where she had been idly separating the peas from the carrots and her eyes seemed anxious.

"Why, Evie? You said you'd stay all summer."

"Well, I just thought. . . ."

"There's a lot yet to do in the shop," Tom said, a trace of alarm in his voice, as though Evie were all that was holding them together.

And so she stayed.

The house was extraordinarily quiet. Occasionally a friend of Donna Jean's would drop by. But Chris was gone, Sue was visiting in Boston, and Matt did not come. Perhaps he had felt that Evie needed to be alone, and perhaps it was true. Several times, however, she had put her hand on the phone to call home, to thank him for what he had said at the graveside. And each time, she imagined Aunt Ida answering, or her mother, or—worse yet—her father. To them, she did not know what she would say.

She did not know, in fact, what she would say to Matt other than thank you. Of all the people there, he alone—for that one moment—seemed to know her best. With quiet compassion, he had done something she could not do for herself. She wondered sometimes if she had ever hated Matt at all, or whether it was something inside herself that even God, she had thought mistakenly, could not love.

Each day that passed in the still house seemed worse than the one before. Evie would go into the shop after breakfast and putter about, but Donna Jean never came to see what she was doing. When Tom was home, the silence became heavier still, like a blanket covering them all—a web, a snare. Wherever Evie went—the porch, down the lane, even—it reached out its tendrils and caught her.

Regardless of what she had said to her father, Evie knew that she would be welcome at home and began to long for it. Home was always there, always open to her. She could not ever imagine her parents disowning her, no matter how serious the offense. Just as she could not give up on Donna Jean, her parents would not give up on her. It was this thought, returning again and again, that made her wonder.

She had never before been so contemplative, and she expressed it in the pages of her journal. Of her argument with her father, she wrote:

I had, in effect, asked him to prove that God was there. I wanted an object for my anger, something that I could touch, a God I could accuse and con-

demn. And yet, in spite of everything, something is here. I can't hold it in my hand, but I can sense it. . . .

It was the same something that made her want to make peace with Matt, the something that had almost lured her to her father's arms before she fled, and now—the something that kept her here in this lifeless house, a silent friend to Tom and Donna Jean. She *wanted* to stay, despite her discomfort. She *wanted* to give, though what comfort she had to offer seemed small. Where did this strength, this compassion, come from? It was both beyond herself and in herself. There was no name for it exactly, but for want of something better, she called it God. Whether it could be reconciled with her father's God, she didn't yet know.

On the third Saturday in August, Evie prepared to go home for a day as she had promised, when the preserves were being put up. In early June, Mrs. Hutchins and Aunt Ida made a small batch each of strawberry and blueberry jam; but near the end of summer, when peaches and plums were ripe, vast quantities of jams and jellies were preserved, most of which would be given away when a small gift was called for.

Tom said that he would drive Evie over. She had just slipped on her sandals when, on impulse, she went down to the kitchen where Donna Jean was sitting.

"I'd like to ask a favor," she said. "It's going to be difficult this year putting up the jelly with Sister Ozzie around. She has to have attention every minute, and once we start the cooking, it's hard to stop. Could you come along and keep an eye on her?"

Tom paused in the doorway, listening.

Donna Jean turned away from the window. "You know I can't."

"Why not?"

She shrugged. "I just can't, Evie. I'm not up to it. And Rose is there. . . ."

"Of course Rose is there. She lives there. But she came to the funeral."

Donna Jean turned to the window again. "I don't even know Sister Ozzie. I'd do more harm than good in my condition."

"In *her* condition, she won't know the difference." Evie went over and stood where Donna Jean would have to look at her. "We really need you. I wouldn't ask if we didn't."

Donna Jean hesitated, then finally got up. "Well, I guess I do owe some people favors." She said it flat, with no emotion. "I'll come for just a little while, Evie, but then I'm going to call Tom to come and get me."

"Sure. Even an hour or two would help."

It was a mild day for August, and on either side

of the highway tobacco farmers were out topping their plants so that the leaves below would grow broader. There had never been tobacco on her father's land, but Evie knew what the men were looking for: if, after a few rows, their hands were sticky with tobacco gum, it would be a heavy crop. In a single morning's work, they could predict their profit. But if they came in the house later with their hands barely stained, the wives would silently shake their heads.

Turning up the drive at the Hutchinses' place, Evie felt just a trace of the old excitement of coming home. After the events of the past few weeks, it was a relief to feel anything at all, and she was especially glad to see something she could count on, something that had been here as long as she remembered. Like the end of winter and the advent of spring, the garden always appeared at the back of the house—always in the same place—the bowling alley rows of string beans, alternating with feathery dill, and further on, the beets and cabbages. Over by the old barn, berry bushes sprawled beside asparagus ferns, and neat rows of onions, broccoli, peppers, and okra competed with each other for space. Then, a little further, the corn. . . .

"I've got some work to do back at the house," Tom told them. "Call me when you're ready to come home."

Donna Jean hesitated. "Maybe you should just come by in an hour."

"No, you call, honey. I'll be there."

It was Aunt Ida who saw them first.

"Well, Donna Jean! No sooner did I pray for another pair of hands than the Lord sent you!"

"Donna Jean, it's so good to see you," said Mother warmly. Evie, too, was included in the welcome. What had happened between her and her father, Mr. Hutchins must have kept to himself.

But it was Rose, turning away from the stove where the first batch of preserves was bubbling, who came over and hugged Donna Jean hard, and Donna Jean threw her arms around her neck. They said nothing at first, but when they dropped their arms and looked at each other, they suddenly hugged all over again.

"I'm glad you're here," Rose said. "I'm sorry it took me so long to say that."

"I'm sorry it took me so long to come," Donna Jean said.

"I thought she might be able to keep an eye on Sister Ozzie for us," Evie ventured.

"Sister's watching her cartoons, and we're grateful for every favor," Mrs. Hutchins told them. "Why don't you help us out here a little while, Donna Jean, and then when Ozzie gets restless, you can go to her."

Murphy came into the kitchen carrying a second

bushel of peaches. When he saw Donna Jean, he stopped, his mouth slightly open. She went over to him and touched his cheek. "That was a beautiful box you made my baby," she said. "I didn't have a chance to tell you."

He blushed furiously. "It w . . . as something I w . . . anted to do," he said.

"I know."

There was almost no time to talk at first. Aunt Ida set to work blanching the fruit, rolling off the skins, then passing them on to Donna Jean to pit and mash. Rose was tending the big kettle, adding the sugar and skimming the foam, while Mother lifted sterilized jars from the boiling water and filled each one. They worked in assembly-line precision, with Evie putting on the lids and taking the filled jars to the porch.

"It smells good," Donna Jean said, after a time.

"And tastes even better," said Aunt Ida. "After each batch we wipe out the kettle with a piece of buttered bread. That's the best part."

"Donna Jean," Rose said over her shoulder, "you take some home with you, now. You'll have enough jam to last you three or four winters."

Donna Jean didn't answer. Evie knew that she was struggling to get through a day at a time—an afternoon, even—without thinking of winter. *I can't wait to show Josh his first snow*, she had said once.

"Where's Matt?" Evie asked at one point.

"Oh, he's taken Mr. Schmidt somewhere to get him off our hands," Aunt Ida told her. "Why, the two of them have been going around Branbury like they was on tour or something, and don't the old man enjoy it, though!"

"Help," came a voice from the back bedroom.

"Cartoons is over," Aunt Ida said. "Now Ozzie will want to go to the bathroom and put on her lipstick and take a walk and everything at once, mark my words."

"Evie, you bring her here," Mother said. "Maybe she'd like to watch."

Sister Ozzie was slipping over the edge of the bed.

"Wait a minute," Evie told her, and brought the wheelchair around. Sister Ozzie looked at her hard.

"What are you doing in here?" she demanded.

"I'm Evie. Remember?"

"You the one that ran off?"

"No, that was Wilma. I'm going to let you watch us make jam."

Evie pushed the wheelchair to the kitchen and up close to Donna Jean. The tall white-haired woman stared fixedly at the newcomer.

"Who's this?" she asked. "She the one who ran off?"

"That's Donna Jean, Ozzie," said Aunt Ida. "Now you sit here and watch what we're doing, and we'll give you a taste after a bit."

"My mama made jam," said Ozzie, leaning over

and peering into Donna Jean's face. "My mama made jam, but she's dead."

Donna Jean paused, the blue-handled masher in her hand, and looked at Ozzie.

"Ozzie, you hush!" said Rose.

"My mama's been dead fifty years, they tell me, and I haven't got over it yet."

Evie stood motionless there in the doorway. For a moment, as Donna Jean looked in the old woman's eyes, it appeared she was about to cry. Then suddenly she reached over and put one hand on Ozzie's. "I lost my mama and baby too, and I don't think I'm ever going to get over it either," she said.

And in one of those rare moments when Sister Ozzie seemed lucid, her own eyes softened and she said, "Well, then, that makes us sisters, doesn't it, and I don't blame you one bit for running off."

Donna Jean smiled and exchanged glances with Rose at the stove, and then smiles traveled about the kitchen. Sister Ozzie leaned back and began to hum.

There was a break between the peach jam and the plum jelly, a time for scrubbing out the kettle and getting Sister Ozzie back to her room.

"I tell you what," said Evie, as she and Donna Jean wheeled the old woman to her bed. "I've got to go down in the cellar for some more jars, but maybe I'll get your purse for you, Ozzie, and you can show Donna Jean all that's in it."

Quickly the tall woman scooted back onto the pillows and waited expectantly while Evie got down the black purse from the closet shelf.

It looked like a pregnant cat, the sides bulging. Every time anyone found something that might please Sister Ozzie, it went into the purse, and when the purse was filled, the treasures went into a shoebox there on the shelf beside it. Every few weeks, Mrs. Hutchins replaced the things in the purse with things from the shoebox, and a little later, she would exchange them all over again so that the old woman was always finding new baubles among her favorites. There was a cheap plastic bracelet, a purple-veined stone from Wyoming, a bluejay feather, a subway token, a tiny paper umbrella from a Japanese steakhouse. . . .

Eagerly the old fingers worked at the clasp until the purse sprang open. Sister Ozzie's eyes widened as she lifted out first one thing and then another. And when she held up a green marble, Donna Jean showed her how to turn it against the light, so that the deep streaks of jade showed through, transmitting a fragile spot of color, a bit of magic, onto what had been a mere bedspread before.

Evie had just gone outside and around to the cellar when she saw Matt wheeling Mr. Schmidt up the drive. Matt looked more tanned than Evie had remembered him, his face more square, as though he had become more of whatever he had been before.

"Hi," she called.

Matt approached cautiously.

"Hi." He looked at her warily. "You home to stay or something?"

"No. Just helping out. I brought Donna Jean with me." She waited until he came up beside her and stopped. "Where have you been?"

"On a ten-mile hike with Mr. Schmidt." Matt grinned at the old man. "Sure would have been nice if somebody had thought to put sidewalks in Branbury. We're gonna need new shock absorbers if we keep this up."

Evie leaned over. "How are you, Mr. Schmidt?"

"Hey, Evie, don't shout at him."

"Was I shouting?" She straightened.

"Yeah. Everybody does. He's not deaf. It makes him think people are mad at him, the way they're always yelling."

Evie looked at Matt, then at the old man.

"I'm sorry," she said more softly.

In response, Mr. Schmidt lifted one hand from his lap and offered her a gumdrop from a small box. Surprised, she took one and thanked him.

"We usually stop by the Millers when we go out," Matt told her, pushing the wheelchair over to the shade of the beech tree. "They always have a little treat for him." He sat down on the arm of a lawn-chair. "What have you been doing lately?"

"Nothing much. Chris has gone back to Silver Spring, and Sue's in Boston. I guess you knew that."

"Yeah." He was quiet for a minute. "Well, I could ride over some evening."

She smiled at him. "You know, Matt, I've been wanting to tell you, sometimes you say exactly the right thing. Sometimes you really do."

He looked at her quizzically, then returned the smile. "Will I blow it if I say I could ride over tonight?"

"I wish you would. I'd like that."

Donna Jean did not call Tom to come for her until all the jam had been made. They had eaten a late lunch together on the back porch, the women, surrounded by the gleaming pink and orange jars, the results of a long day's work. By the time Mr. Hutchins came home from church, where he'd gone to prepare his sermon, the kitchen was cooling off, the pans had been washed, and Donna Jean was giving Ozzie a haircut on the back steps.

Evie saw her father getting out of the car beneath the beech tree, heading around the garage to look at his tomato plants, his special pride. She left the others and slipped up behind him just as he was murmuring, "Doggone slugs! Dog-*gone* those slugs!"

She put her hands over his eyes. Beneath her fingers she could feel the wrinkle-lined skin stretching into a smile. He reached up and clasped her hand. "Evie."

She laughed and moved around beside him. "We

made enough jam for the whole congregation," she said. "If you get a jar with sugar crystals in it, that's the batch I made. I got to talking and wasn't thinking."

"A little sweetness never bothered me," he said.

They walked around the edge of the garden, inspecting it together. The rows were carefully weeded and cultivated, Murphy's handiwork. The half-acre of corn beyond was Matt's province.

"I've been thinking about those words we had between us. . . ." Mr. Hutchins said at last.

"So have I."

"It hurt, Evie, I don't deny it. But I'd rather you said what was on your mind than hold it back."

"I can't apologize for the questions, Dad—maybe for the way I asked them. But they needed to be asked. Maybe we're not so far apart in our feelings."

He nodded. "What seems clear to me from where I stand, honey, may not seem clear at all to you, and you got to call things as you see them. The important thing is we're in this life together, and we shouldn't forget that." He put his arm around her as they started back to the house. "Sure is nice having you home, even though I know it's not to stay."

"It'll be soon," she said. She could not promise him more than that, more than that she was coming home. She knew he would not press her.

In the car going back, Donna Jean leaned against

the seat and looked up at the trees, as though seeing them again after a long absence.

"You know, Tom, when I went up the walk to their house today, I dreaded them looking at me, as though my face had been crushed along with my heart. But then, working beside them, listening to that old lady. . . ."

Tom glanced over, waiting.

"I've been so awful to live with, thinking I'm the only one who's ever been hurt in her life."

Tom pulled her to him, and she rode the rest of the way with her head against his shoulder.

When they stepped inside the house, there was a surprise. Tom had spent the day working on their shop. The last of the counters had been mounted on legs and varnished, and the floor had been swept. Only the painting of the walls remained.

Donna Jean and Evie stood staring from the doorway—Evie exclaiming and praising. In her mind's eye she could see the bolts of calico and gingham resting there on the tables, the pottery and wood carvings on the shelves behind, woven baskets hanging from hooks on the ceiling, and patchwork quilts with "Star Flower," "Bear Paw," and "Churn Dasher" designs, decorating the huge expanse of wall on one side.

Tom beamed. "I've been busy, too."

But Donna Jean was cautious. "We don't have much to put on the shelves," she said finally.

236

"We will."

"I don't think I'm up to driving around looking."

"We can wait."

But still she hesitated. "It won't take the hurt away, Tom."

"I know."

"Well. . . ," she sat down finally in the doorway to stare some more. Tom and Evie crouched down beside her, putting their dream into words—where this would go, where that would be. . . .

The yellow cat, which had followed them indoors, came brushing up against each of them in turn, purring. When it came to Donna Jean, it seemed to pause, uncertain. This time, she leaned back and let it crawl into her lap.

Fifteen

SITTING SIDEWAYS ON THE BAR, her legs
stretched out at an angle, Evie squealed as the bike
wobbled down the highway, then careened into the
lane.

"Matt!" she screamed as it headed for a tangle of
blackberry bushes, corrected itself, and then—
geared for disaster—plunged across the road in the
opposite direction, coming to rest in the honeysuckle.
Evie found herself catapulted across the handlebars,
tumbling over and over down the slope.

She could not stop laughing. Matt came scrambling down the hill after her, a piece of vine trailing
behind one ear, and the sight of it set her off again.
She lay on her back, knees doubled up, and shrieked.

"You okay, Evie?" he kept asking, and nudged
her with one foot. "You okay?"

She quieted at last, her hands on her stomach.

"Of course I'm okay," she gasped. "Oh, Lord, Matt, it feels so good to laugh."

"You looked like you were having a fit or something." He was still holding the sack of doughnuts they had bought at Hollander's. "Come on. Let's eat."

She got up, following him over to the flat marble tombstone, and they sat facing each other, legs crossed in front of them.

"Should have got some soda, too," said Matt, carefully taking a bite out of the chocolate doughnut. He made a face at a sheep that was munching nearby and licked his fingers.

School was only a few days off. But there were still things to be done. They had spent several evenings tramping around Branbury looking for something that Donna Jean could use to make baskets. They found some willow and birchbark along the creek, but not nearly enough.

As soon as word got around that Donna Jean Rawley was up to making baskets, however, someone from the lumberyard had driven up one morning and dumped a pile of white oak splits on the Rawleys' porch and then driven off before anyone could get out of bed to thank him. They were heavy, quarter-inch splits, and Donna Jean had stared at them in grateful disbelief.

"She still think about Josh all the time?" Matt asked.

"Well, of course! Why on earth wouldn't she?"

"I know she *misses* him," said Matt, "and every time she thinks about him, it hurts. But she'll get to the place where she's not thinking about him all the time. Some day she'll be busy doing something else, and she'll think, Hey, for a while I forgot about Josh. And then there will be longer spaces between the remembering."

"How do you know so much about it?"

"Because that's the way it was with Dad. When he left, I mean." Matt took the empty doughnut sack, blew it up, and popped it. The sheep bolted across the cemetery. "That's what it was like when he left us. Just sudden—like an explosion. I always wondered if it was better that way, instead of him hanging around, quarreling with Mom. Maybe he did it because he thought it would be easier on me."

"That was probably it," said Evie. She watched him curiously, then rested her chin on her knees, arms around her legs. "I want to tell you something, Matt, and if you ever blab it to a soul, may your tongue rot."

He didn't answer, just waited.

"When Donna Jean was in labor, when it really started to hurt, she said she didn't want the baby."

"So?"

"So look what happened."

"You think that made it happen?"

"It makes me wonder."

"Not me. If every time we said something it came true—wow! What a mess. You're not magic, you know."

"I wasn't thinking of that. I was thinking of God."

"Oh."

"It's going to be hard for me to go to church again, Matt, with all these doubts."

He stared at her. "You never had any before?"

"I never knew I did. Then *you* came along. . . ."

"Holy Moses, what do *I* know?"

"Sometimes you talk like you know it all."

"Evie, I don't know *anything*. Why do you think I ask all the questions?"

"But some people never worry about what they believe—they honestly think they have all the answers."

"Huh-uh. I don't buy that. Anybody who thinks he has all the answers never had any questions. Or else he's too scared to admit it. You've heard of the Inquisition, I suppose."

"What's that got to do with it?"

"It just shows how freaked out people can get when they have doubts. They want everybody to believe like they do, because that reassures them. Anyone who disagrees, he gets the rack and the thumbscrews. We don't use thumbscrews anymore; we just talk about hell. Anybody who doesn't believe—well, just wait till the Last Judgment, buddy, and you'll get yours. Heck, how can you *help* but have questions if you're only a speck in the universe?"

She thought it over, her face intent. "What about my father and what he believes? What if he's wrong?"

"Evie, for Pete's sake, how are you ever going to know? Doesn't the way he lives his life count for anything?"

"You never had anything good to say about the way he lives his life," she shot back.

This time it was Matt who was silent. "I've got this habit . . ." he said at last. "Sometimes, when I meet people for the first time, I look for all their faults. I don't want anything to come out later, to take me by surprise. After I've figured out all the reasons why I shouldn't like them, I get around to figuring all the reasons why I *should*. Sometimes it takes a while."

She watched him and began to smile. "Same with me. Sometimes it takes a whole summer, practically."

He smiled back.

They walked toward the bicycle.

"Did you ever make up your mind about college?" he asked.

"I think I'll go—work in the shop part-time. What about you?"

"College, I guess. Haven't seen any ads for ranch hands in the paper lately." His shoulders rose in the familiar slouch. "You and Chris going to get married?"

"Lordy, Matt, I haven't even graduated from high school yet."

"I just mean, are you thinking about it?"

"Well, I sure haven't made any arrangements. I'm not even sure I *want* to marry."

"Me, either."

"But then, when I'm thirty, I suppose I'd panic. That's what happens to women, you know. They call it the biological clock. A woman reaches thirty without having children and an alarm goes off or something."

"Yeah. I guess if I ever did want to get married I'd do it before I was so old my kids would think I was their grandfather."

They reached the bicycle and Matt picked it up out of the vines and straightened the handlebars.

"You want to ride?"

"Think you can get me there in one piece?"

"You don't wiggle around on it, I can."

She hoisted herself up on the bar again as Matt steadied the frame. And then they were moving down the lane, the breeze in her face, her hair blowing back against him.

"I tell you what," Matt said, his words coming jerkily as he pedaled. "Let's make a pact; no matter where we go, we'll keep in touch, and if we're still single when we get to be thirty, we'll think about marrying each other."

"Matt Jewel, you're just the craziest—!"

"I didn't say we'd marry, I just said we'd think about it. When we get to be thirty."

"Do I have to sign it in blood?" Even without looking, Evie could tell that Matt was smiling, could visualize the way his lips turned up at the corners.

"No," he said, "just tell me it's not completely unthinkable."

"It is certainly within the realm of possibility," said Evie. "How's that?"

"It's enough," said Matt, and rode her gently to the porch.